THE TWELVE THIEVES OF CHRISTMAS

ROSIE DARLING

CHAPTER 1

"$\mathcal{C}$ome away from that window, Jack." Mary Talbot snatched her younger brother's arm and pulled him away from the glass. She looked around nervously but could see nothing other than crisp white snow and huge snowflakes falling gently to earth. London seemed to have vanished behind a blanket of white. Even the constant rattle of carriages had been silenced by the heavy snowfall. An eerie quiet had taken its place.

Mary shifted uncomfortably, eyes darting around the dark grounds of the large white townhouse. At the sight of the candles flickering in the window, Jack had darted instinctively through a gap in the wrought iron fence to look closer, leaving Mary with little choice but to follow.

"I ain't doing nothing but looking," Jack hissed back at his sister. The little boy had to stand on his tiptoes to peer into the lavish candlelit room beyond the glass. "They're having roast chicken," he said indignantly. "It's still three days to Christmas and they're having roast chicken already. No wonder that fellow is so fat."

Despite herself, Mary couldn't help looking over her brother's shoulder to peek through the window. She couldn't disagree with Jack's assessment of the gentleman sitting at the head of the table. His stomach was so round he could hardly pull himself up to the polished wooden table in order to eat the meal. A well-dressed lady sat beside him, cutting her meat into pieces and popping them delicately into her mouth. Mary assumed she was the man's wife, although the couple weren't speaking. The lady kept her eyes straight ahead, seemingly to avoid her husband's eye. If Mary had to guess, she would have said the lady had been forced into marriage by her parents. An advantageous marriage was everything to the wealthier classes. Love didn't matter when there was money involved.

A woman in servants' clothing was circling the table, serving potatoes, carrots and gravy to accompany the roast chicken. Mary salivated as she imagined tucking into the feast. In the corner was a Christmas tree decorated with holly and little red candles. Ever since that drawing had appeared of the Queen and her family around a Christmas tree, no well-to do-family could do without one.

Sitting at the table with their parents were two well-dressed children; a boy and a girl around the same age as Jack and Mary. However, whereas Jack and Mary were street urchins dressed in whatever oddment of clothing they could find or steal, these two children were immaculately attired. The boy was almost a copy of his fat father in a tweed jacket, waistcoat and red neck cloth. He even had a start of a paunch around his middle. The blonde-haired girl wore a dress of pure white lace that had probably taken a month to make. It had probably cost more money than Mary had ever seen in her life. Their mother looked at them adoringly and the little street urchin felt a pang of jealousy.

How Mary missed her mother.

She had died six years ago, giving birth to Jack. Five years later, their drunken brute of a father had followed her to the grave, leaving the orphaned brother and sister to fend for themselves on the streets.

Mary had heard horror stories about the workhouses and orphanages. How they kept families apart. How they caned you for the slightest mistake. She swore to herself she would avoid them at all costs.

"We're going to be all right," Mary had promised her little brother, though at just nine years old, she was terrified. She squeezed his tiny hands. They felt cold in hers. "We're going to stay together and that's what's important."

Jack had looked her in the eye and nodded, and Mary knew he believed her. She swore then and there she would do everything in her power to keep her little brother safe. She would even give her own life if she had to.

They had sold anything of value in their tenement, which was little, and left on the morning the rent was due. Mary knew their father's death had probably saved their lives. Most nights, he had come home drunk and regularly beat the pair of them. He had given Mary little money for food and then hit her for not putting enough to eat on his dinner table.

She didn't miss him at all.

Mary stamped her feet on the ground in a desperate effort to try and get some warmth into them. The snow was now at least an inch thick, and starting to cover their footprints. She wondered how deep it would be by the morning.

She tugged her brother's arm again. "Come on, Jack. They're gonna be on their guard in that house. I'm cold and I want to get home."

"Just one more minute."

"No! It's time to go," Mary shouted a little too loudly. The weather had forced the majority of people inside and they were the only ones on the street. Her voice rang out, destroying the silence. She saw the fat fellow look up towards the window and his face immediately reddened. He shouted something she couldn't make out but he pointed directly at her brother. The man stood up with not an inconsiderable degree of effort and headed for the doorway.

Mary snatched her brother's hand and the two tried to dart awkwardly towards the gap in the fence. Their worn boots slid on the icy surface, slowing their progress. Mary heard the click of the front door cut through the stillness. The fat gentleman waddled down the stairs.

"Stop, urchins!" he bellowed. "What in God's name are you doing?" He started to stride through the snow towards them.

Mary panicked. "Quickly, Jack." Grabbing her skirts in her fists, she hoisted herself over the fence.

Jack skidded on the fresh snow and crashed into the black wrought iron fence. He steadied himself after a second and began to squeeze through. For one horrifying moment, Mary thought he was going to get stuck. But Jack was as thin as any other street urchin on the streets of London. Just as the fat man reached him, puffing heavily with sweat dripping off his brow, he managed to wriggle through the gap.

The man's face was now puce with anger. "You swines! You thieving little swines." He paused for a moment, gulping down his breath. "Police!" he hollered.

A younger man in a butler's uniform had appeared from the doorway and was running down the gravel path towards the large iron gates. "Apprehend them, Martins," the fat man instructed his butler. "These could be the ones."

Martins was held up for a few seconds while he

lifted the heavy bolting mechanism that kept the garden gates firmly shut.

"Police!" the fat man bellowed again, his harsh little eyes darting. "Police!"

Mary pulled on Jack's threadbare jacket. "Run!"

Hand in hand, they turned and fled. They reached the end of the street and whirled around to see that Martins was continuing the chase. The fat man had clearly given up, leaving the task to his servant.

Jack turned right, heading towards the tenements and slums of Whitechapel. It was a busier road and people were going about their business despite the weather. None of them stopped to look at the fleeing children. Such a sight wasn't unusual.

They skipped carefully around the hot chestnut seller who was packing up his stall for the evening. They almost knocked his remaining box of chestnuts over in the process. He shouted an insult after them.

Martins wasn't so lucky.

His polished butler's shoes weren't faring well on the snow. On this busier street, it had been compacted underfoot by the passing pedestrians and had turned icy. The chestnut seller was still staring and shaking his head after the disappearing children when he pushed his cart directly into Martins' path. The butler skidded straight into it ended up in a heap on the floor.

Jack and Mary turned at the sound of the crash. The chestnut seller was waving his arms wildly, giving their pursuer a dressing down. Jack burst into laughter but Mary tugged his arm, urging him to continue running.

"Come on," she said panting heavily, "we're not safe yet."

The children continued running down the road before turning down a small alleyway that no gentleman would dare venture into. Mary glanced over her shoulder but saw no sign of Martins – or worse still, a policeman.

Finally, they stopped in an alleyway that led to the slums. They rested their backs against a damp brick wall and took huge gulps of the freezing air. Mary's lungs were burning and her legs felt like lead. She closed her eyes for a moment. That had been far too close for comfort. And for what? They'd not stolen a thing; not a loaf of bread to feed themselves or jewels that could be sold, or even a few pennies to buy chestnuts from the seller's wagon.

She flashed a wild glare at her brother. "Next

time I tell you it's time to go, you listen to me," she hissed. "Do you understand?"

Jack looked down, ashamed, and nodded. After a moment, he dared to look up, giving her a tiny smile. "Did you see the way that butler went flying, though? Weren't it brilliant?"

"It's not funny," Mary snapped. "He would have caught us if the chestnut seller didn't get in the way."

Jack continued to giggle. "But he—"

Mary felt a sudden anger tear through her. Before she knew what she was doing, she had slapped her brother across the face. His eyes widened in shock. Never once had she laid a hand on him. She felt instantly ashamed, as though she had far too much of their father inside her. But Jack had to learn.

"I'm sorry," she said, her voice shaking slightly. "But this ain't something you ought to be laughing at, Jack. Do you want to get hanged?"

"Hanged?" Jack repeated. "I'm only six! They don't hang boys as young as me."

Mary wrapped her arms around herself. "Well. You'll be old enough soon. So we need to learn to be careful now. Or else one day it'll be too late."

Jack said nothing, just stared downwards,

chewing his lip. Mary felt a pang of regret. She hadn't meant to scare him. She'd only meant to teach him a lesson. She put a gentle hand on his shoulder and reached into her pocket to pull out the silk handkerchiefs she had stolen that day. She handed them to her brother.

"Here. Take them. They'll need sorting when we get back."

Jack nodded again but still didn't speak. With her hand still on his shoulder, Mary began to walk, leading him back towards their tenement.

CHAPTER 2

Their building was the last in a row of five; a miserable, run-down shell of a place with five crooked storeys disappearing up towards the cloud bank. A faint light glowed behind the boards and cloths that covered the windows, and smoke curled from the chimneys of those lucky enough to have heating.

Jack and Mary climbed the stairs to their third-storey room and let themselves inside. The ten other orphans who lived there were already inside. The single room was filled with chatter, the fire crackling in the corner giving the place a much-appreciated warmth. Mary shrugged off her wet coat and gratefully held her numb fingers to the flames.

"You're late," crowed Maggie, ushering everyone to the table in the centre of the room. At eighteen, Maggie Shaw was the oldest of the group and had taken on the role of mother to the eleven children. Though Mary knew better than to trust Maggie completely, she could not deny that it was nice to be taken care of a little. And that pot of potato stew Maggie was lifting from the hook above the fire did smell delicious.

"You ain't usually late," Maggie continued as she began to spoon the stew into bowls. "Did you run into trouble?"

Mary decided it was best not to tell Maggie about their run-in with the fat man and his butler. "Nothing we couldn't handle." She slid onto the wooden bench at the table, her shoulder pressing against her friend, Bobby Taylor. He flashed her a smile.

Mary glanced at Jack, ready to give him a warning glare to keep him from telling Maggie about their adventure. But he was already shovelling the stew hungrily into his mouth, the fat man with the roast chicken seemingly forgotten.

Maggie sank into her rocking chair at the head of the table and lifted the bottle of gin that lived beside the chair. All the others knew better than to go near it. Maggie had once caught Lizzie Moore sneaking a sip from the bottle and had slapped her until she cried. She yanked out the cork and took a long gulp.

For several moments, there was no sound but the gentle tapping of wooden spoons against the side of the bowls. The coals shifted noisily in the grate.

"Snow was real heavy today, weren't it," David, one of the oldest boys spoke up after a moment. "Bet it lasts until Christmas."

"I love it when it snows at Christmas," one of the younger girls said with a smile.

"All right for you, Rose," Bobby chipped in. "You ain't got holes the size of Africa in the soles of your boots."

Mary flashed Bobby a knowing smile. Her stockings were still cold and damp from their tramp across the city. What she wouldn't give for a new pair of boots.

"Right then," Maggie said brassily when most of the bowls were empty, "let's see what you've all brought me today."

One by one, they went around the table, pulling from their pockets the trinkets they had stolen during their day of picking pockets. Harry Simon produced a studded hair comb and Rose had managed a silver bracelet. Lizzie and her twin brother David both had handfuls of gold coins. When it was Mary's turn, she handed Maggie the engraved silver pocket watch she had stolen from a gentleman outside the theatre earlier that evening.

Maggie held it up, examining it in the flickering light of the lamp. "Oh yes," she said, tossing her dark curls out of her eyes with a flamboyant flick of her head. "Lovely. This'll make sure we have a nice feast on Christmas Day."

Mary lowered her gaze. Although picking pockets was a matter of survival for them all, she couldn't escape the shame of it. Nor could she escape the constant feeling of dread that followed her at the thought of how easily any of them could end up in the gallows.

"And what about you, Master Jack?" Maggie asked with a warm smile. Jack was the youngest of all the children and was clearly Maggie's favourite. Though Maggie's erratic behaviour made Mary nervous at times, she was glad the older girl cared for her brother.

Jack reached into his pocket and produced the silk handkerchiefs Mary had given him earlier. "I sorted them and everything," he announced proudly. "These ones are silk, and these are linen, but they're embroidered all pretty."

Maggie smiled broadly. "And what a fine job you've done. I'm sure they'll fetch a few pennies."

Jack beamed, clearly relishing Maggie's praise. "And," he said, "in that house we robbed last week, well, they got brand new silver! We saw it through the window!"

Mary's stomach lurched. She tried to shoot Jack a glare from across the table but his attention was focused on Maggie.

Maggie tapped a long finger against her chin. "Silver?" she repeated.

Jack nodded eagerly. "Silver knives and forks. To replace the ones we stole. Me and Mary saw them eating roast chicken with it. The man was so fat!" He laughed boisterously, earning a giggle from nine-year-old Catherine.

"How interesting." Maggie eyed David and Brian, the two oldest boys. "You fellows had no trouble breaking in there last time, did you?"

David gave a snort of laughter. "Easy as anything. Their butler was a right fool. Didn't even know we was in the house til we was on our way back out the window."

Jack broke into a fresh round of giggles,

earning a kick on the shin from Mary. He stopped laughing at once and looked down, chastened.

Maggie took another gulp from the gin bottle. "Well then. It's settled. We'll pay the old fat man another visit. On Christmas night when he's too stuffed to move!" She broke into boisterous laughter. "We'll be the twelve thieves of Christmas!"

Laughter rippled across the table but Mary didn't join in. She and Jack had only narrowly escaped the house. Going back there felt like tempting fate. But she knew speaking to Maggie about her concerns would get her nowhere. The older girl was bold and brash and rarely listened to anyone. There was no danger to their thieving, Maggie liked to say, because they were so good at what they did. Mary knew her concerns would just be laughed off.

Still chuckling to herself, Maggie grabbed her coat from where it hung on the back of the rocking chair and slid it over her shoulders. She pulled a woollen bonnet on over her wild curls and slid all the stolen trinkets into a cloth bag.

"Right then," she announced brassily, "I'm off for the night. See yourselves off to bed. We've a big day tomorrow – people out and about for Christmas. Plenty of pockets for you all to get your hands in." She gave a loud cackle.

The door creaked loudly and then thumped shut, and Maggie's footsteps disappeared down the stairs. Every night she did this – vanished off into London to exchange their stolen goods for money. Mary had no idea where she went or who bought the items, and she was glad not to know. On most nights, Maggie returned long after midnight, stumbling into the room with liquor on her breath. Strange men would come to their door at all hours of the day and night, demanding to speak to Maggie. She'd whisper and giggle with them in the doorway, her voice low so none of the children could hear what was being said.

With Maggie gone, Tracy Drew, who was the next oldest, got to her feet and clapped her hands together. "All right then. You all heard Maggie. Let's get this mess cleaned up and get ourselves to sleep."

In a well-practised routine, the children gathered the supper dishes and washed them in the bucket of melted snow one of the boys had gathered earlier and heated by the fire. They stacked the bowls and spoons in the corner of the room, ready to be used the next day and then unrolled their straw sleeping pallets that stood up against the wall. Tracy blew out the lamp, leaving the room lit only by the muted glow of the fire.

Mary lay awake for hours, listening to the gentle snoring of the other children. Jack lay curled up beside her, his eyelids fluttering in sleep.

"You all right, Mary?"

She turned at the sound of Bobby Taylor's murmur. She was glad to see him awake.

When she and Jack had first arrived at the tenement six months ago, Bobby had been the one to make her feel most at home. Mary and her brother had been out picking pockets at Covent Garden when a hand had grabbed her from behind. Mary had whirled around in a panic, expecting to see the police. Instead, it was Maggie's grinning face looking down at her.

"I've got just the place for you," she'd said. She winked. "I'll teach you how to pick pockets properly." Though she had no desire to learn to pick pockets properly, Mary knew she had little choice but to go with Maggie. After all, picking pockets was the only hope children like her had of getting a little food in their bellies. Besides, after months of sleeping in alleyways and under shop awnings, the bed and warm fire Maggie spoke of sounded like heaven. Nonetheless, there was a part of Mary that was terrified. What was she getting herself and Jack into? But when she arrived at the tenement and received a warm smile from Bobby Taylor, she felt a few of those anxieties slip away.

"Can't sleep," she told him now.

Bobby got to his feet and climbed awkwardly over the other sleeping bodies until he reached Mary's side. She shuffled across her sleeping mat to make room for him.

"Is something wrong?" he asked.

Mary sighed. "This robbery Maggie's got planned for Christmas night. I got a bad feeling about it."

"Why?" Bobby asked gently.

Mary shrugged. Logically, she knew this robbery was no more dangerous than any of the other thefts they attempted. But she couldn't shake the feeling of foreboding that hung over her. "Just don't feel right," she said finally. "Me and Jack hardly got away last time. Their butler chased us all the way into the city."

"Maybe you should tell Maggie."

"Tell her what?" said Mary. "That I got a bad feeling? She'd just laugh in my face."

Bobby nodded faintly in agreement. He

grabbed Mary's arm as footsteps sounded towards the door. "She's back," he hissed.

Mary closed her eyes, feigning sleep.

Bobby gave her arm a squeeze. "It'll be all right, Mary. I know it."

But Mary knew he could make no such promises.

CHAPTER 3

*C*hristmas Day came all too quickly. While the other children were excited about the day, Mary couldn't shake the feeling of dread over the upcoming theft that evening.

"Just wait til you see the feast we're gonna have today," Bobby told her that morning in what Mary knew was an attempt to take her mind off her worries. "Every Christmas Maggie makes sure we eat like kings."

As promised, that evening, the table was laid with more food than Mary had ever seen in her life. An enormous goose took pride of place in the centre, surrounded by gravy and potatoes, ham and vegetables. Despite herself, Mary's mouth started to water. Every scrap of the feast had been purchased with stolen coin, of course, but at that moment she couldn't bring herself to care. Even in the days before her parents had died, they had never had more than a few scraps of rabbit on Christmas Day.

The children dived in eagerly, filling their plates and shovelling the food down as though it might be taken away from them at any moment.

"This is the best food I ever had in my life," Jack told Mary, his mouth half full of ham.

Mary couldn't hold back a smile. Maggie's feast had certainly lived up to expectations. She just wished she could enjoy it a little more. Wished this gnawing fear at the back of her mind would settle. No one else at the table seemed to be worried about Brian and David's upcoming adventure. Then again, no one else had seen the black-eyed eagerness with which the butler had chased them down the street. Except for Jack, of course. And he was far too busy with the ham and potatoes to worry about such things.

When the food was finished, Maggie stood up ceremoniously. "Gifts!" she announced. "Gifts for everyone!"

Mary straightened in her chair. Gifts? She had never imagined this celebration might also include gifts. She'd never received a Christmas present in her life. Her heart quickened with excitement.

Behind the rocking chair, Mary saw then, Maggie had hidden a stack of packages all tied up in cloth and ribbon. She handed one to each of them.

"Merry Christmas, all of you," Maggie said warmly, punctuating her greeting with a mouthful of gin. She slapped the bottle noisily back on the floor.

Each package contained a few items of clothing – coats and gloves, or shirts and dresses. Some of the children even had new boots. Mary unfolded the blue woollen skirts Maggie had given her. She ran her finger over their thick fabric. They would be far warmer than the patched and threadbare dress she had been existing in for the past year.

"Thank you," she said to Maggie.

Maggie flashed her a smile. "Of course, love. Got to keep you all warm and clothed, don't I?"

And yet Mary couldn't help but wonder to whom these skirts had previously belonged. Had they been bought new? Stolen from a seamstress's parlour, or perhaps the second-hand stall at the market? Was their previous owner dead?

She pushed the thought from her mind. She

was in no place to be choosy about the clothes she wore.

On the other side of the room, David and Brian were pulling on their new coats. They were about to head out into the night to steal the silver from the fat man's house.

"I feel like a gentleman," said David with a grin, buttoning the coat to his neck. "We'll fit right in around Kensington."

Mary kept her eyes downcast. She couldn't look at them. "Do you really think this is a good idea?" she blurted suddenly, the words falling out without her having any thought of it. Everyone turned to stare at her. But Mary was glad she had spoken up. It went some way to easing the restlessness inside her.

As expected, Maggie responded with a boisterous laugh. "Course it's a good idea, love. You saw that silver yourself, aye? Imagine how much food that could buy."

"But the butler. He chased—"

"Don't you worry about the butler," David cut in. "We can outrun him in our sleep. Can't we, Bri?"

Brian nodded. "Course we can. We did it last time. I told you, he didn't even know we was there."

"Besides," said Lizzie, "me and Tracy are gonna go keep an eye out. Yell out if the coppers show themselves." She put her hands on Mary's shoulders and looked into her eyes. "So you don't got nothing to worry about. All right?"

Mary managed a tiny nod, but before she could speak again, the four were heading for the door, giving a boisterous wave to the group as they left.

* * *

DAVID MOORE CHARGED off down the street, Brian, Lizzie and Tracy scrambling to catch up with him. His heart was thumping with anticipation, a warm buzz inside his head from the ale Maggie had served up at Christmas dinner.

What could be better than this? An enormous meal to celebrate the season, and a little jaunt to the side of town where the toffs lived to snatch a few pieces of silver from people who had too much. David chuckled to himself as he walked.

"What's so funny?" asked Brian, slightly breathless after jogging to catch up with him.

David shook his head. "Nothing. Just thinking about the look on the face of that skinny little butler when he saw us climbing out the window last time. Looked like he'd seen a ghost."

The others laughed.

"Poor little Mary Talbot's afraid you're going to do something foolish," said Lizzie.

Brian shook his head. "That girl worries too much. Always bothered about something, ain't she."

"I think it's sweet," said Tracy. "She just don't want to see you getting into trouble." She looked at David pointedly. "Maybe she's right. Maybe you should stop being so cocky and watch yourselves."

David slung an arm around her and squeezed. "Where's your sense of fun, Tracy? It's Christmas, after all! And what better way to spend it than to have ourselves a little thieving? Some nice silver cutlery will look mighty fine on our supper table."

Tracy laughed. "Yes," she said with a wry smile. "And I'm real sure Maggie will let you keep them."

David winked. "Just for the night, maybe. So we can all pretend we're toffs."

It was close to midnight, and the city was settling into a heavy silence after a day of celebrations. Occasionally, a cab rattled past, wheels sighing through the wet snow on the road. Lamps glowed in a few windows but many of the houses were in darkness, save for the starry glow of Christmas candles that speckled the dark.

David stopped walking. He pointed up at the fat man's house. "This is the one."

Lizzie's eyes darted back and forth across the street. "There's no one around. Didn't see one single copper on the way over here neither." She looked at Tracy. "You?"

Tracy shook her head.

"Good," said David. He looked at Brian. "You ready?"

"Ready."

David turned to Tracy and his sister. "Watch the street. If you see anyone coming, yell out."

The girls nodded. A well-practised routine. They had all done it many times before.

David and Brian made their way to the corner of the fence where the wrought iron was bent enough for a boy to fit through. David squeezed himself through with difficulty.

He chuckled to himself. "Too much ham."

Brian gave a snort of laughter as he followed David through the fence. "Next time we're sending Bobby and Harry out here. We're getting too big for this."

The two boys crept through the snow towards

the large window at the front of the house. David knew from experience that the window led directly into the large dining room. He also knew from experience that the lock on the window could be jiggled in just the right way for it to come free. He and Brian would slip inside as silently as ghosts, steal the cutlery from the kitchen, and be back at the tenement long before dawn.

David reached for the window latch. One shift to the side, one jerk to the left. And a short, sharp rattle in its casings. Just as it had on their first visit to the house, the window slid smoothly open. David heaved himself through the opening, landing on soft feet inside the dining room. He stepped aside, allowing Brian to follow.

The house was silent and dark, the stillness punctuated only by the ticking of a grandfather clock somewhere in the hallway. David motioned silently for Brian to follow him deeper into the house. He remembered the place well. Navigated through the passages towards the kitchen with barely a wrong turn.

Faint moonlight shone through the window of the kitchen, lighting up the cooking pots left upturned on the rack to dry. The last of the orange embers glowed through the door of the range. The smell of roast meat and vegetables hung thick in the air. David smiled crookedly to himself. Whatever the fat man and his family had eaten for Christmas dinner, he was sure it wasn't half as good as the spread Maggie had put on for them today.

He glanced around the moonlit room, his eyes falling on a large sideboard against one wall. He nodded towards it. "In there."

He and Brian crept towards the cabinet, sliding open the drawers and peering inside. They were cluttered with place mats and matches, candlesticks and serving utensils. And there, poking out of a length of cloth, were the items they had been searching for. David reached into the drawer and pulled out the bundles of silver cutlery, sliding them into the deep pockets of his coat.

He flashed a smile at Brian and then the two boys began to tiptoe back towards the open window.

As they stepped into the dining room, a sudden creak of the floor made them whirl around. David's blood ran cold. Because there in the shadows was the fat man's butler, a pistol held threateningly in front of him.

* * *

ANXIOUS AS SHE WAS, Mary was tired after the enormous meal, and soon she was sleeping fitfully on the floor with the other children. Her dreams were punctuated by chestnut sellers and girls in lacy dresses, and running through the snow, pursued by an invisible attacker.

A sudden wail cut through the stillness and Mary sat up in the darkness, yanked from sleep. She gulped down her breath, disoriented by the frightening dream and the horrifying cries that still echoed in her ears.

Maggie fumbled in the dark for the lamp and when she lit it, its pale glow fell on the figures of Lizzie and Tracy in the doorway. Lizzie was wailing uncontrollably while Tracy stood with her arm around her, trying in vain to comfort her.

"What happened?" Maggie demanded. "Where are the boys?"

Lizzie cried harder.

"They got caught," Tracy said, her voice beginning to waver. "Me and Lizzie, we was watching the street real carefully but that butler, he must have heard them in the house. He came into the dining room and stood there waiting for them. We didn't have no way of telling David and Bri he was there." She wiped away a stray tear. "The fat man sent for the coppers and they took the boys away."

Lizzie broke into a fresh round of sobbing and Tracy pulled her into a tight embrace, Lizzie's cries muffled against her shoulder.

Bobby met Mary's eyes across the room. She chewed her lip. She felt cold and hollow inside. And yet she could not pretend to be surprised.

She turned away from the older girls, unable to look at the anguish on Lizzie's face. She couldn't imagine how it would feel to know her brother was in the hands of the police. Mary found herself shuffling closer to Jack. She closed her eyes and curled up on her sleeping pallet, trying to block out the painful reality.

But there was no escape from Lizzie's traumatised sobbing. And when the first hint of dawn appeared through the cloth covering the window, Mary gave up trying to sleep.

ON NEW YEAR'S DAY, David and Brian were to be hanged. That morning, a stilted silence hung over their lodgings. Lizzie had barely spoken since her twin brother's arrest, her eyes constantly red and swollen. Mary could barely look at her. The thought that it might one day be her brother walking to the scaffold was far too real and raw.

Maggie and the two older girls pulled on their coats without speaking. They had all been forbidden to attend the execution. Mary was glad of it. She had never seen a person killed and she couldn't bear to see Brian and David die.

The three girls left without speaking. For a long time, no one spoke. Catherine and Rose sat together with Jane Tuesday, the three crying softly while Harry and Bobby busied themselves emptying the grate and refilling it with fresh coal.

Jack crawled across the floor and sat up against the wall beside Mary, looping both his arms around one of hers. Mary began to stroke her brother's hair; an effort to calm herself as much as him.

"You see?" she said finally, her words catching in her throat. "This is why we gotta be so careful. This is why we can't do anything foolish. You understand?"

Jack peered up at her, his big blue eyes wide. "I understand," he murmured. "And I'm gonna be real careful from now on. I promise."

CHAPTER 4

*T*wo years had passed since the ill-fated burglary at the fat man's house in Kensington. David and Brian had not been replaced and nine children now sat on the floor of the tenement, looking up at Maggie and waiting expectantly for her to start speaking.

A great Christmas racket, Maggie had called it. A plan that would see them feast like never before on Christmas Day. And would see them in warm clothes and sturdy boots all year round.

"Got my hands on some Christmas trees," she began, swaying back and forth in her rocking chair. "A hundred and twenty of them, to be precise."

Mary exchanged glances with Jane Tuesday

who was sitting beside her. Where on earth had Maggie come by a hundred and twenty Christmas trees? Still, she knew better than to ask questions.

"We sell 'em to the toffs," Maggie continued. "Even offer to decorate them and everything."

"Decorate them?" Rose repeated. "You mean we take the trees into the toffs' houses and pretty them up in there?"

"That's right," Maggie grinned. "And while we're in there, we keep our eyes out for any little treasures we might take out in our pockets. Good plan, eh?"

Rose nodded obediently.

"What about me and Lizzie?" asked Tracy. "You want us involved in this too?"

"Course not," said Maggie. "You and Lizzie got more important things to do."

For the past year and a half, Lizzie and Tracy had been going out to the streets, selling their bodies to the city's men. Though the thought of doing such a thing made Mary ill, the two older girls constantly bragged about how much money they earned. Mary was infinitely grateful she would be selling Christmas trees instead. She knew it was only a matter of time before Maggie sent her out to sell herself.

Two days later, the children lined up at the washbin and scrubbed themselves clean, ready to head out into the streets to sell the trees.

"Won't be doing this for much longer," Jane said to Mary as they buttoned their dresses. She grinned proudly. "Soon I'll be going out with Lizzie and Tracy. Making some real money; Maggie said so."

Mary chewed her lip. "And you're happy about that?"

"Course I am," said Jane. "You ought to hear some of the stories Lizzie and Tracy tell about the things their clients give them. Bracelets and necklaces and all kinds of things. Maggie even lets the girls keep some of them." Her blue eyes shone. "Can you even imagine such a thing! Having jewels all of your own?"

No, she couldn't imagine it. And the promise of jewels did nothing to ease her dread about one day being sent out with the other girls. The thought of letting a man touch her like that made her stomach roll.

She shook the thought away. She couldn't bear to think of it now. Today, she would just focus on selling Christmas trees.

The children followed Maggie downstairs and

out into the alley behind the tenement where a forest of pine trees seemed to sprout from the muck of the gutters. Bobby was pacing back and forth as he guarded them, blowing on his hands to keep them warm.

"Any trouble?" Maggie asked him.

Bobby tossed his dark hair from his eyes. "Couple of fellas were curious about where we got them and all. Told them to mind their own business."

Maggie nodded. "Good. We'll take these five with us today. I'll have some more for us tomorrow."

Carrying five Christmas trees from Whitechapel to Covent Garden, Mary soon discovered, was no easy feat. Even for eight of them. The roads were lined with old, icy snow, and the trees were dreadfully awkward to carry. Jack and Catherine, the two youngest children, had been loaded up with bags of decorations. They contained an endless array of ribbons and glass beads, candles and colourfully wrapped sweets. Once again, although Mary was endlessly curious about where Maggie had found such things, she knew better than to ask.

By the time they reached the marketplace,

Mary was exhausted and a line of sweat was running down her back. Her legs were aching and they had not even begun the workday yet.

Maggie nodded to a corner of the square in full view of the market. "We'll set up right there. Where everyone can see us." She winked at the others. "Just you wait; we'll be the centre of attention. Christmas trees are so popular these days that every one of these toffs will want our services."

They hauled the trees into the corner and leaned them up against a wall. "Christmas trees!" Maggie called into the square. "Get your Christmas trees right 'ere! Decoration included!"

Just as Maggie had predicted, their service caught the eye of many of the well-to-do folk strutting across the square. They gathered around Maggie and the children, inspecting the trees, dressed in their fine woollen gowns and greatcoats.

Instinctively, Mary's eyes pulled to the gold watch chain hanging from a man's coat. On any other occasion, she would have grabbed it in an instant, with the poor man being none the wiser. But not today. On the walk across town, while they'd grunted and grumbled under the weight of the trees, Maggie had warned them that today was not about thieving.

"That will come later," she'd assured them. "But first, we got to seem like good, honest workers. It's the only way the toffs will let us into their houses." Her grin widened. "And that's when the real thieving will begin!"

Less than an hour after they had set up their stall, they had sold their first tree. Maggie clapped her hands together, summoning everyone's attention.

"Right then. Mary and Bobby, you carry the tree to the gentleman's house. Jack will come with you with the decorations. The rest of you stay here."

"What about you?" Mary asked.

Maggie grinned. "I'm coming with you." She dropped her voice. "You could use a sharp pair of eyes. Check the place out. See if it's easy pickings."

Mary felt the familiar lurch of dread in her stomach. So this plan of Maggie's wasn't just about selling Christmas trees and pilfering little trinkets from the wealthy people's houses. It was about finding the homes that would make for an easy burglary. Mary felt a tug of resentment. Had

Maggie not learned a thing from David and Brian's deaths?

Nonetheless, she grabbed one end of the Christmas tree and followed Maggie across the square. What choice did she have but to do what the older girl said? If she questioned her or refused to do as she asked, Mary knew she would be out on the streets before she could even fathom what was happening. Reckless though Maggie was, Mary knew she was her only hope of a little security. Her only hope of a roof over her head.

She looked down at Jack who was walking beside her, clutching the bag of decorations. With his unruly blond hair combed and his grimy face scrubbed clean, he almost looked like a different boy. "Keep your eyes open," she told him. "And don't do anything stupid. You just concentrate on decorating the tree. Leave the thieving to the rest of us."

Jack nodded obediently.

The gentleman's house was not far from the square. The butler opened the door for them and ushered them into an enormous entrance hall. The was painted bright white, with portraits dotting the walls. A large staircase rose from the foyer with a neatly-carved bannister of dark polished wood. The man who had bought the tree stood waiting for them. He was rather young, with neat dark hair and kind brown eyes.

"This way," he said, his voice low. "I thought it would look wonderful in the parlour. Right over here." He gestured to the corner of the room. He looked at the children, giving them a conspiratorial smile. "If you could keep rather quiet, that would be wonderful. I'd like to surprise my wife with the tree once it's decorated." His eyes shone with warmth.

"Don't you worry," Maggie agreed in a whisper. "We'll be quiet as a mouse." She flashed an overly bright smile and ruffled Jack's hair. "Won't we now?"

Jack nodded while Mary hovered awkwardly beside him, trying to swallow down an all-too-familiar feeling of dread.

Maggie and Bobby set the tree into its stand and slid it into the corner. The man was right, it was a wonderful place for it. Carefully, they began to decorate it, winding the strings of beads around the branches and dotting the fronds with coloured sweets and sprigs of holly.

On the edge of her vision, Mary could see a small crystal candleholder glinting on the mantelpiece. Nothing too extravagant, but it would surely fetch a small sum. But she pulled her eyes away, pretending not to have noticed it. The young man had been so warm and friendly, and he was clearly excited about surprising his wife. Mary hated the thought of tainting that with their thieving.

But Maggie nudged her sharply in the shoulder. "Hey. We ain't here just to decorate trees, you know," she hissed.

Mary sighed inwardly and nodded. She moved around the side of the tree closest to the mantel and reached up, swiftly grabbing the candleholder. It felt heavy in her pocket. Almost as though it was weighing her down.

The door swung open and the man's dark head poked inside.

"Oh!" he exclaimed. "It looks wonderful! Come inside, darling. Come and look." He stepped inside the parlour, tugging the hand of a pretty blonde woman.

She looked at the Christmas tree and her eyes lit up. "Oh, Thomas!" she cried, whirling around to face her husband and clasping her hands together at her chest. "It's perfect! Thank you so much." She turned to the children. "And thank you, all of you. You've done a wonderful job."

Mary felt tears of guilt pricking behind her eyes.

* * *

"WELL," said Maggie on the walk back to the square. "That was hardly worth it now, was it. One miserable candleholder. Show it to me, Mary."

Mary took it from her pocket and handed it to the older girl. She was glad to be rid of it.

Maggie turned the smooth ornament around in her hands. "Crystal," she noted. "Good quality at least." She slipped it into her own pocket. "In any case, I had a good chance to get a proper look at the place. Found the best way to get in and out. I'll send Harry back there in a few days."

"No!" Mary cried suddenly, the word escaping without her having any thought of it.

Maggie looked at her, her dark eyebrows raised. "What?"

Mary swallowed. "Those people seemed so nice," she said. "Do we really have to rob them?"

She was expecting an angry outburst, but Maggie just sighed and reached a motherly arm around Mary's shoulder.

"Oh, Mary," she said with a sigh. "Haven't you

learned by now that there's no place for conscience in this game? We just can't afford that. If we felt guilty every time we stole from someone who looked a little friendly, we'd all starve to death. I'm sorry, but that's just the way it is."

Emboldened by Maggie's unexpected kindness, Mary said, "Aren't you worried that Harry will get hanged? Just like David and Brian were?"

"What happened to David and Brian was an accident. Harry knows better than to let it happen again." Maggie let her arm fall from around Mary's shoulder. "Honestly, Mary, you need to harden up a little. Anyone would think you were brand new to this game. Don't you know by now we got no choice in the matter? You want food on the table, then this is the way it has to be."

CHAPTER 5

*B*y Christmas Eve, only one Christmas tree was left. It was the smallest of the bunch, with uneven branches and a fat, gnarled trunk. Mary knew they had little chance of selling it.

She stamped her feet, trying to get some warmth into her toes. Sleet was blowing across the square, stinging her cheeks and causing her to squint in the half-light. Mary was glad this racket with the Christmas trees was nearly over. Since they had started selling them, she and Jack had been to at least twenty houses, pocketing whatever trinkets they could find. She always left with a feeling of guilt firmly settled on her shoulders. Stealing from people after they had let them into their house, she had come to realise, was far worse than simply picking pockets in the street.

She had felt the guiltiest when Harry had returned from robbing the house of the young man and his wife. She had been lying awake on her sleeping mat when Harry had returned to the tenement. She heard Maggie gushing profusely over the takings but just lay there with her eyes closed, pretending to be asleep. She wanted no part in the crime. Wanted to pretend it had never happened.

She blew on her hands again, jumping up and down to keep warm. She glanced over at Maggie. Surely it was time to accept this last tree was not going to be sold. Surely it was time to head back to the tenement for Christmas Eve. Then she noticed an older man approaching. He was tramping awkwardly through the snow and seemed to be in a hurry.

"This all you got?" he asked, eying the tree with disdain.

Maggie nodded. "Yes sir. Everything else has been sold. And we don't got any decorations left either. So it's just the tree for sale."

The man stood for a moment in hesitation. He sighed, then finally, he nodded. "I'll take it."

When he had disappeared out of the square, his

footman carrying the tree over one shoulder, Maggie turned to the group. "Well then," she said brightly, "that's a hundred and twenty Christmas trees sold! I think we ought to have a side of ham tomorrow to celebrate!"

"And potatoes and gravy!" Rose put in. "Can we have potatoes and gravy, Maggie? Please?"

"Of course."

"And plum pudding—"

Catherine stopped talking suddenly. Because approaching them was an older woman with a face like thunder. At her side was a policeman. Mary's stomach knotted. She recognised the woman. They had visited her house in Knightsbridge a few days ago.

"That's them!" the woman hissed, pointing a gloved finger in their direction. "They stole my silver picture frame. With my dead husband's portrait in it!"

Mary glanced sideways at Jack. She knew exactly which picture frame the woman was talking about. She had warned Jack against taking it, as the woman would likely notice it missing right away. And yet, that evening, when they had sat around the supper table and produced the day's takings, Jack had pulled the frame from his pocket and handed it proudly to Maggie.

He looked up at her with wide, fearful eyes. Mary bit her lip. She wanted to scold him, but what good would that do now? How many times had she warned him against foolish behaviour?

Maggie stepped forward to speak to the woman. "Do you have any proof of this?"

"These children were in my house last Tuesday," she snapped. She pointed at Jack and Mary. "These two. They were there to decorate the Christmas tree."

Maggie held her icy gaze. "And do you have any further proof that they stole the picture frame?"

"Further proof?" the woman repeated bitterly. "Of course I don't have any further proof! I wasn't in the room at the time." She turned to the policeman. "Surely you can see these urchins are guilty!"

Maggie stepped up to the policeman and murmured in his ear. Mary couldn't catch all of her words but she heard her mention *my best girl*. The policeman's eyes flickered for a moment and then he stepped back and cleared his throat.

"I'm sorry, ma'am," he said to the old woman, "but I'm afraid you just don't have enough proof of this theft for me to make an arrest."

Mary felt her shoulders sink in relief.

"This is outrageous!" the woman cried. "Who else could it possibly have been?" She huffed dramatically, then charged back across the square, shaking her head and mumbling to herself.

Maggie gave the policeman a brusque nod and then gestured for the children to follow her out of the square.

By the time they reached the tenement, Mary's heart was still racing. Jack had apologised to her at least ten times on the walk home.

"It's all right," Mary told him. "But you need to learn from all this. Next time I tell you not to do something foolish, you listen to me."

Jack nodded and chewed his lip. Mary could tell he had learned his lesson.

While they sat around the table eating their stew that night, Tracy combed her hair and put on her best dress. Though no one had said as much, Mary knew she was being sent to the policeman. Maggie's *best girl*. The thought sickened her. But Tracy seemed to be taking pride in being labelled the best. She peered into the tiny shaving mirror Rose had stolen on one of their Christmas tree decorating sessions, pinned her dark hair neatly at her neck, and dabbed scarlet-coloured salve to her lips.

She stood up, facing Maggie. "How do I look?"

Maggie gulped down a mouthful of gin, letting the bottle swing by her side. "Like you'll make that nasty copper forget all about young Jack's light fingers."

TRACY PULLED her coat around her and hurried out into the street. The weather was just as dreadful as it had earlier in the day. The wind whipped across the streets, beating her skirts against her legs. Shards of ice stung her cheeks, and she pulled her hood down low to avoid her hair becoming wind-blown. The neater and more professional you looked, she had learned early in this game, the more money your clients were willing to pay.

Not that she'd be getting any money for this little jaunt. No, this was all about ensuring those coppers kept away from Jack and the others. Tracy didn't mind. Not really. The other orphans in Maggie's thieving ring were the closest thing she had to a family. And she knew any of them would do the same for her.

Her evening with the policeman passed uneventfully. He had been awkward and shy about the whole encounter, and Tracy could tell he was not the kind of man who usually did such a thing. When they were finished, he'd shunted her out of the hotel room with red cheeks and an embarrassed goodbye. Still, she knew he would not come after Jack or any of the others again. She knew he wouldn't risk her opening her mouth and telling anyone what had passed between them.

Tracy pulled up her hood and began the long walk back to Whitechapel. She was exhausted, craving a few hours of sleep. She was also looking forward to Maggie's Christmas feast.

"Hey. You there." The gruff male voice made her whirl around. A young man was leaning against a street lamp, bringing a pipe to his lips. The smoke curled upwards, disappearing into the silver black sky.

Tracy recognised the man as a client of hers although she couldn't remember his name. She remembered he had been rough and crude-mouthed and stank of cigar smoke and filth. She gave him a brusque nod and kept walking.

"Where you going, lass?"

Tracy quickened her pace at the sound of his

footsteps sloshing through the snow behind her. He reached out and snatched her arm, pulling her back to him roughly.

"I'm talking to you." His fingers tightened around her elbow and he gave her a yellow-toothed smile, blowing a cloud of pipe smoke into her face. "What say you and I have a little fun?"

Tracy shook her head, trying to pull away. "I'm finished for the night. I'm going home."

The man chuckled. "No, you ain't."

Her heart began to speed. She had trained herself not to fear her clients; these questionable men she spent her time with. Pushing aside that fear was a necessity. But there was something about this man that made her breathing quicken and the blood rush in her ears. Something about him that made the skin on the back of her neck prickle with dread.

For a brief moment, she hesitated. Maybe it was best to just go with him, let him have his way with her, and be done with it. She was about to open her mouth to agree to a half-hour with him, but something held her back. She couldn't do it. Her instinct told her to run. Run as far away from him as she could.

Before she could think on it any further, she

burst into a clumsy sprint, slipping on the ice and scrabbling with her hands to right herself. She heard the man's cold laugh behind her and then his footsteps approaching once again.

Fear clouded her vision and made the snow-covered city spin. She felt that rough hand back around her elbow. Felt him pulling her towards him. And then she felt a sudden, violent blow to her head and the world around her disappeared.

WHEN MARY AWOKE on Christmas morning, the room was already a hub of activity. Maggie, dressed in brightly coloured patched skirts, was barking instructions to Harry and Rose about the collection of a ham from somewhere in Stepney. Jane and Lizzie were sitting at the table chopping a pile of vegetables that seemed to have appeared from nowhere, and Bobby and Jack were stoking the fire, ready for the chaos of cooking that was to ensue.

Mary rubbed her eyes and sat up on her sleeping pallet. She was surprised she had managed to sleep through so much noise.

"Good morning, sleepyhead," Jane called down at her. "Come and help us with the vegetables."

Mary obediently joined them at the table, taking a knife from the box on the shelf to help them peel the potatoes. She looked around the room. "Where's Tracy?"

Lizzie shrugged. "Don't know. I ain't seen her since she went off with that copper last night."

Mary frowned. "Ain't you worried about her?"

Lizzie shrugged. "She can take care of herself. She probably found another client, is all." She looked at Jane and giggled. "Maybe it was that fat old judge that wants to marry her. He's probably got her tucked up in some fancy hotel somewhere, feeding her wine and chestnuts."

Mary didn't return her smile. When she had last spoken to Tracy, the older girl had been raving about how much she had been looking forward to Maggie's Christmas celebrations.

"Tracy said she were looking forward to getting her gift from Maggie," Mary said in a small voice.

"Gift from Maggie?" Lizzie repeated with a laugh. "Believe me, girl, she'll be getting far better gifts from that old toff." She leaned forward to speak to Jane and Mary in a whisper. "Last time she saw him, he gave her a bracelet with a real diamond in it. She hid it from Maggie, of course." Lizzie shot a furtive glance at Maggie across the room. "Ain't no way she was letting her get her hands on it."

Perhaps Lizzie was right, Mary told herself, as she peeled the potatoes and chopped them into pieces for boiling. Maybe Tracy had simply found someone willing to give her diamonds and chestnuts and take her to a fancy hotel. After all, Lizzie knew far more about these things than Mary did. But she was unable to shake off her unease.

Later that afternoon, the table was laid with the ham, potatoes and gravy, along with plum pudding, sweets and jellies that strange men who claimed to be friends with Maggie had delivered to the door.

Mary did her best to enjoy the extravagant meal. But the food did little to take her mind off the fact that Tracy had still not returned home.

"Shouldn't Tracy be back by now?" she asked Maggie quietly while they ate. "It's not like her to miss Christmas dinner."

Maggie just laughed. "She probably got a better offer! Found a few drunks with money to fill her pockets. What do you think, Lizzie?"

Lizzie laughed. "You still on about that, Mary? I

already told you, she's fine. Trust me." She shook her head with a sigh. "Just enjoy your dinner. Ain't every day we get to eat like kings."

* * *

THE NEXT MORNING, Mary woke early. She sat up on her sleeping mat and peered around the room of sleeping bodies to see if Tracy was among them.

"She's still not back," said Bobby from behind her.

Mary turned to face him. "You're worried too?"

"A little," he admitted. "Maybe Maggie's right. Maybe she did find new clients. But maybe…"

"Something else happened," Mary finished.

Bobby nodded.

Mary pushed her tangled blonde hair from her eyes. "I can't help thinking about Brian and David at this time of year," she told him. "So maybe my mind's just playing tricks on me. Making me think the worst."

Bobby stood up suddenly and held out his hand. "Come on. Let's go for a walk. The city's so peaceful at this time of the morning. Besides, it will do us good to get out of here for a while. Might help us stop worrying."

Mary smiled in agreement. She grabbed her coat and boots and followed Bobby down the stairs and out into the street.

After days of bleak, snowy weather, the morning sky was clear, the first hint of sun breaking over the horizon. Mary lifted her face upwards, feeling faint rays against her cheeks. It felt as though she hadn't seen the sun in weeks. The gentle warmth went some way to ease the feeling of dread in her stomach. Maybe her mind really was playing tricks on her, and she ought to stop fearing the worst. In all likelihood, Tracy would be home tonight, bragging to Lizzie and the others about how much money she had made in the Christmas spirit.

She and Bobby walked out of Whitechapel and down towards the river. The streets were near-deserted, the city no doubt recovering from its celebrations the day before. The shouts of a news-paper seller on the corner seemed to cut through the cold air.

At the sight of the newspapers, Mary stopped walking. She had never learned to read properly, but could nonetheless make out one of the words in the headline: *Dead.*

She pointed at the pile of papers at the seller's

feet. "What does the headline say?" she asked Bobby.

He shrugged, then pointed to two women on the corner. They were each reading from the front page and chatting among themselves. Curiously, Mary edged closer.

"Excuse me," she asked the women in a tiny voice, "could you tell me what the story on the front page is about?"

One of the women sighed wistfully. "Oh, it's quite dreadful. A young lass was found murdered on Christmas morning. They're saying she was a working girl. Probably killed by her client."

"No one knows who the poor girl is," the second woman added. "We'll probably never even know her name."

Mary felt sickness rise in her throat. She managed a nod of thanks to the women and then stumbled away. Tears spilt down her cheeks. "It's Tracy," she coughed. "I just know it."

Bobby put a gentle hand on her shoulder. "You don't know that for certain, Mary. You heard what the papers said – they don't know who the girl is."

But there was no doubt in Mary's mind. She knew their little group of orphans was now down to nine.

CHAPTER 6

*M*ary never stopped thinking about Tracy. One year passed, and then another, and still she couldn't shake the older girl's disappearance from her mind.

Disappearance. That was what Bobby called it whenever Mary raised the subject with him. But she knew the truth. Tracy had not simply disappeared. She had been murdered. And the man who did it would never be brought to justice. Because who cared about a murdered street urchin? Especially one who made a living selling her body.

Maggie had never openly acknowledged Tracy's death. She had told everyone she had run off to a better life with a man who spoiled her with treasures and kindness. On many occasions, Mary had tried to convince herself that it might be true. But she could not make herself believe it.

Christmas was approaching and Maggie had them all out on the streets regularly, picking the overflowing pockets of London's well-to-do. Mary was glad she had not revisited the Christmas tree racket from two years earlier. Whenever she thought about those days, she shuddered, thinking about how close Jack had come to facing the hangman.

She knew her younger brother held himself to blame for Tracy's death. After all, had he not been caught stealing the picture frame, she would never have been sent out into the streets that Christmas Eve. Over and over, Mary had tried to convince her brother that it was not his fault; that no one was to blame except the man who had killed Tracy. But she knew Jack was not convinced.

Although Mary always hated having to steal, she felt a particular heaviness on her shoulders at this time of year. Far from partaking in the joy of the season, Christmas always made her fear the worst.

"What about Maggie's Christmas dinner?" Jack would say to her. "Ain't you looking forward to that? And what about the gifts we get? It ain't every day someone gives you a pair of new shoes!"

Mary knew he was right, and she did her best to return his smile. But Christmas only reminded her of David and Brian's hanging. Reminded her of sitting at the dinner table waiting for Tracy to appear, and yet knowing deep inside herself that she never would.

In the week leading up to Christmas, Mary noticed the streets had become a little quieter. In the streets around their tenement, people began to whisper about a new outbreak of cholera.

"I don't want to go out working tonight, Maggie," said Lizzie at supper one night. "One of my clients last week told me his housekeeper got sick and died."

"I heard the baker what sells those giant bread rolls got it," Harry added.

Maggie waved a dismissive hand. "So what? You're all gonna stop working just cos a few people got sick? I don't think so. The rent don't stop. So neither will we."

"We got enough money to pay the rent, surely," Bobby spoke up. His eyes met Maggie's. "Maybe we ought to stay home for a while."

"Stay home?" Maggie repeated. "In the three

days before Christmas?" She gave a snort of laughter. "It'll be our busiest time. Everyone's carrying bucket loads of money around so they can put fancy food on their tables."

"It won't be our busiest time if all our customers are getting sick and dying," Harry murmured under his breath.

Maggie shot him a glare. "What did you say?"

He shook his head. "Nothing."

Maggie scooped up the last of her stew and tossed the spoon back into the bowl. "Nothing changes," she said. "Lizzie and Jane, you two will go out tonight and see your clients as arranged. The rest of you will be back at the market in the morning. And I expect to see a decent haul tomorrow night." Her voice hardened. "Do you understand me?"

Around the table, heads nodded mutely.

"Besides," said Maggie, forced brightness in her words, "it's Christmas. No one gets sick at Christmas."

THE FOLLOWING DAY, the children went back out into the streets just as Maggie had ordered. As they walked through the slum in the direction of the market, Mary could hear wailing coming from several of the buildings. Families huddled together on street corners, cheeks drained of colour and dotted with sweat. Fear glowed in people's eyes. Mary could tell several of them were already ill. There were few passers-by on the streets.

The wealthier parts of town were quiet too. The market was far less busy than it usually was in the days before Christmas, and those who came did not linger. Nonetheless, the children were such proficient pickpockets that even the briskest of passers-by could fall victim to them.

Jack had become the most skilled of them all; able to swipe a man's money clip in a heartbeat without the victim having any thought of it. Each night, he was the one to produce the most around the supper table. The one who made Maggie's smile the brightest. Mary didn't know whether to be proud or horrified.

Mary and Jack were the first two to return to the tenement that day. Though they had lost sight of the others early in the morning, the two siblings made sure they always stuck together. Mary hated the idea of her little brother thieving – and she hated, even more, to think of him out on the streets alone. Jack was ten now, the same age Mary had been when they had first come to live with Maggie and the others. But Mary knew she would always think of him as a precious little boy, and she would always do everything she could to look out for him.

She knelt to light the fire, hunching over the grate and holding her hands up to the tiny flame to warm them. As much as she hated thieving, she knew it was what paid for their coal, and for that she was grateful. She couldn't imagine how dreadful it would be to live without so much as a fire.

The door swung open, revealing Rose, Catherine and Harry. The two girls headed straight for their sleeping pallets, while Harry looked on with a deep frown.

Mary got to her feet. "What's happened?"

"They ain't well," said Harry. "Last night, I heard Catherine saying to Rose she didn't feel good. When I was out at the market, I found her sitting up against the wall outside the cobbler's. She said she was too sick to stand. I barely managed to get her home."

Mary's stomach rolled. Catherine was curled

up on her sleeping pallet, her thin blanket pulled up over her face. Mary heard a muffled groan.

She turned to Rose. Her cheeks were flushed, and her skin pale. "You're not well either?"

"I'm just thirsty," Rose managed. "I'm so thirsty."

Mary tried for a smile. "We'll find you some water." She put a gentle hand to Rose's shoulder. "Lie down and rest. You'll feel better soon." She tried to force a steadiness into her voice.

Her eyes met Harry's in an unspoken question. *Is it cholera?*

Mary had little thought of it. Had no idea about the illness and its symptoms. All she knew was that Rose and Catherine needed help.

She went to the shelf for the flask of water Maggie kept there. It was close to empty. She took it to Rose and knelt beside her. "Here. Drink a little."

"Mary," Harry called from across the room, "maybe you shouldn't get too close."

Mary shook her head. "They need help. I ain't going to just leave them."

Out of the corner of her eye, she could see Jack shifting nervously in front of the fire. "Be careful, Mary," he murmured.

Mary took the bottle from Rose and took it to Catherine's sleeping pallet. She pressed a hand to the girl's shoulder. Catherine replied with a low moan.

"Catherine," Mary said gently, "I've got some water here. You ought to drink some. It might help you feel better."

Catherine's only response was another groan.

The door swung open and Bobby stumbled into the room, collapsing warily on the bench beside the table. His hue was deathly pale.

Mary looked up. "Bobby? Are you all right?" Her heart began to speed. *Please, not Bobby too. Please.*

He smiled at her, but Mary could tell it was forced. "I'm all right," he said. "Just a little tired."

Mary frowned. His cheeks were flushed and his breathing was rapid. She blinked back her tears. This couldn't be happening.

She took another sleeping mat from where it rested against the wall and laid it on the floor beside Rose and Catherine. "Lie down and rest," she told him, giving him a forced smile of her own. "I'll bring you some water."

Without argument, Bobby dropped onto the sleeping mat and pulled his knees to his chest.

Mary hurried back to Catherine's side and took the bottle.

"Please," Rose coughed, reaching a hand out to Mary as she passed. "I just need a little more."

"Bobby needs some water too," Mary said gently.

Rose nodded weakly, closing her eyes.

Mary hurried back over to Bobby. She held the bottle to his lips. "Here. Drink this. You'll feel better soon, I promise." She could hear the waver in her voice. She blinked away her tears and turned to her brother. "Fetch us some more water."

Jack nodded obediently and grabbed his coat, disappearing out of the room without another word. Harry hurried after him, murmuring something about helping.

Flustered, Mary moved between the three sick children, doing all she could to make them comfortable. Perhaps they were just tired, she tried to tell herself. Worn out from the long hours Maggie had them working. But her feeble attempt at optimism was futile. She felt certain it was cholera. Catherine's agonised moans left her in no doubt.

Footsteps sounded outside the apartment,

echoing in the stairwell. Mary turned back to Rose. "That'll be Jack. With more water for you."

Rose replied with a muted groan. But when the door flew open, it was Maggie standing before them. She planted her hands on her hips, looking down at the three children.

"What's going on here?" she demanded. "Are they sick?"

Mary's stomach lurched. "Just a little tired," she said, her voice coming out thin. "I told them to lie down and rest."

"Tired?" Maggie shook her head. "Don't you lie to me, Mary. Don't you dare." She looked at the three groaning bodies, and then back at Mary. "Is it cholera?"

"I don't know," Mary mumbled, unable to meet Maggie's eye.

Maggie nudged Catherine with her toe. "Get up. Catherine. Rose." Another kick. The two girls groaned.

"What are you doing?" Mary demanded. "They need to rest!"

"They need to get out!" Maggie snapped. "They ain't staying here and getting the rest of us sick!" She shoved her boot into Bobby's shoulder. "Up you get. Right now. On your feet."

Bobby sat up, his eyes wide. "Maggie, I—"

"On your feet!" she snapped. "Get out of here! This second!"

Mary's tears spilt. "No, Maggie, please. You can't."

"They're going to die anyway," Maggie hissed. "And they ain't taking the rest of us with them!" She kicked hard against Rose's hip, forcing her to roll over. The younger girl got shakily to her feet, pulling Catherine up with her.

"Please, Maggie," Mary said again. "Please…"

Bobby looked at her with watery eyes. "She's right, Mary," he said. "We got to go. Or the rest of you…" He reached for his coat, unable to finish his sentence.

Mary's tears spilt. She stumbled to her knees, sobbing into her hands. She wanted to grab Bobby's hand and pull him back. Wanted to plead with him to stay. But somewhere deep inside her, she knew he was right.

"And you," Maggie snapped to the girls. "Out."

Catherine opened her mouth to speak but said nothing.

"Did you not hear me?" Maggie hollered. "I said out!" She reached beneath her skirts and produced a pistol, brandishing it in the direction of the two girls.

Rose let out a shriek, while Mary's sobbing intensified. Catherine reached for Rose's hand, and the two girls stumbled towards the door. Rose looked back over her shoulder at Mary.

"Thank you," she mouthed.

Mary squeezed her eyes closed, unable to watch them leave.

BOBBY STUMBLED down the staircase of the leaky tenement. Behind him, Rose was in tears, while Catherine groaned loudly in pain.

"It's going to be all right," said Bobby, doing his best to offer a smile. But he knew his words were of little comfort to the girls. He didn't even believe them himself. How could he? They had nowhere to go, nothing to eat, nothing but the clothes on their backs. He felt feverish and dizzy, and he doubted Catherine would survive the night.

He slowed down a little, wrapping an arm around her waist to help her stand. They stumbled weakly down to the bottom of the staircase.

Bobby stood motionless for a moment, hesitating to open the heavy wooden door that led to the outside world. Once they stepped through it, they were truly on their own. And he knew there could be few outcomes other than death. He only hoped it would be quick and as painless as possible.

He closed his eyes for a moment. If he listened carefully, he could still hear Mary sobbing in their room three storeys above his head. The sound of it made him ache. Mary was the dearest friend he had ever had and leaving her was even harder than stepping out into the snow to face his death.

In spite of his pain, he knew Maggie was right to do what she had. He knew if they had stayed, all the children would likely fall sick. Many of them would have died. And Bobby could not bear that. He sent a silent goodbye to Mary and, with all his remaining strength, heaved the door open.

"Where are we to go?" Rose coughed, stumbling on the icy bank outside the tenement. She shivered violently, trying to pull her ratty coat tighter around her body. Bobby glanced at her to see that the colour had completely drained from her face. Her eyes were red-rimmed with tears and fever.

"We need to find shelter," Bobby managed,

ignoring the sudden violent pain in his stomach. "Somewhere to rest."

And without any idea where he was going, he began to walk. What else was there to do? Perhaps they would find an abandoned building or an overhanging awning that might offer a little shelter.

But when Catherine finally fell to her knees and declared she could not go any further, they were in the middle of an alley on the edge of Whitechapel. A cluster of people was gathered at one end of the street, huddled around a small fire. Its meagre glow lit their pale cheeks and sent sparks darting into the darkening sky.

Bobby eyed the fire longingly. His every muscle was aching and his fingers and toes were numb with cold. He craved a little warmth on his skin. But he knew what would happen if they tried to approach. One look at the three children would tell anyone they were riddled with cholera. They would be banished, chased away like rabid dogs.

Bobby put a hand to each of the girls' shoulders and tried to usher them around the corner into an even smaller lane. Here, the discoloured snow was thick on the ground and barely indented with footprints.

Bobby sank to his knees, too exhausted to go further. He had little idea of where they had walked to but knew they could go no further. He tried to gather the girls around him. Perhaps they could find a little warmth, a little comfort in each other. But Catherine was already curled up on her side, her eyes fluttering as she groaned in pain. Rose was on her knees beside her friend, tears flooding down her cheeks.

Bobby reached out and squeezed her hand. Then he let the exhaustion pull him down and closed his eyes against the snow.

"HONESTLY, MARY," said Maggie at supper that night, "would you stop looking at me like I were the devil himself? You know I had no choice." She took an enormous swig from the gin bottle. "If I hadn't thrown them out we'd all be dead."

Mary didn't answer. She used the back of her hand to wipe away her tears; tears that hadn't stopped falling since Bobby and the girls had left the building. Maggie was the closest to a mother any of them had. How could she have been so cold and heartless?

Did she feel an ounce of regret, Mary wondered? In all the losses they had suffered – David, and Brian, and Tracy, and now Bobby and the girls – Maggie had never hinted that she might be feeling any grief. Was she truly so cold-hearted, Mary wondered. Or was she simply good at hiding her emotions beneath her brassy exterior?

She tried not to think of what Bobby and the girls were doing right now. She hoped they had found somewhere warm and dry to at least take shelter. Perhaps they would even recover, she told herself. But she couldn't make herself believe it. She knew that in all likelihood, Bobby, Rose and Catherine would die curled up in the streets of the slums like so many other forgotten urchins.

No, she corrected herself. Not forgotten. They would never be forgotten. Nor would David, and Brian and Tracy. Maggie may act as though their lives were expendable, but Mary swore to herself she would always remember them.

Jack leaned over to murmur in her ear. "You ought to eat something."

Mary looked down at her untouched bowl of stew and nodded faintly. She tried to smile at her brother. Jack was no longer the helpless little child he had been when they had first come to live with Maggie. These days, he looked out for Mary as much as she did for him.

She brought the spoon to her lips and forced down a mouthful. The food stuck in her throat and she pushed her bowl away. Maggie looked up from her rocking chair, her dark eyes narrowed.

"You're not sick too, are you?"

"No," Maggie murmured. "I'm not sick. I'm just not hungry." She stood up abruptly. "I'm going to sleep."

The other children looked on with wide eyes. No one ever left the supper table until Maggie told them to.

"Mary," Jack murmured. "Sit down."

But Mary looked defiantly at Maggie. She knew she was being foolish. Knew there was every chance Maggie would throw her out into the street like she had done with Bobby and girls, whether she was sick or not. But right now, she was too overcome with grief and anger to care. She reached into her pocket and pulled out the single watch she had managed to steal that day. It was old and tarnished and she knew Maggie would get little for it. The thought pleased her somewhat. Maggie didn't deserve a thing after the way she treated the children who were supposedly in her care.

Her care.

Mary almost laughed at the thought. She'd believed that at first when she and Jack had first come to live here; believed that Maggie cared about them. But she saw now that that belief had only come out of desperation. She had wanted to believe Maggie would care for them, love them, and mother them because there was no one else to do so. But it had never been about that. All they were to Maggie was a means to making money.

She dumped the watch on the table without saying a word. Didn't wait for Maggie to comment on it. Then she took her rolled-up sleeping mat from against the wall, set it up in the corner and lay down, closing her eyes against the bitterness of the world.

A SENSE of despondency hung in the air of the apartment as they ate their Christmas dinner the next day. There were just six of them here now; half the number there had been on that first Christmas Mary and Jack had spent at the tenement. Despite the reduced number, Maggie produced just as much food, piling the table high with meats, vegetables and lavish puddings. But no one ate much.

None of them except Maggie. "Come on, all of you," she crowed. "Let's see a smile or two. It's Christmas Day! And look at this fine feast I've brought you!" She snorted, swinging back wildly in her rocking chair. "I say it's about time you all started to show a bit of gratitude. Where would you all be without me?"

No one spoke.

Mary felt the emptiness of the seat beside her that Bobby usually filled. She rubbed her eyes, feeling an ache deep inside her. And she lay her head on her arms amidst the overflowing bowls of their Christmas feast, far too exhausted to cry.

CHAPTER 7

*M*ary carried her bitterness towards Maggie throughout the next year and the next. A need to leave the tenement was beginning to take root inside her. She couldn't bear to live her life risking the hangman each day for Maggie Shaw's benefit. But where was she to go? She had no skills, no money… As much as she hated to admit it, Mary had to admit the truth – without Maggie, she was lost.

"Are you all right, Mary?" Jack asked as her they let themselves inside after an afternoon picking pockets outside the theatres. The room was cold and dark, with no one else inside. These days, everyone came and left as they pleased. The shared suppers were a thing of the past. Nowadays, they just handed their takings over to Maggie whenever she reappeared and demanded them. Mary was still none the wiser as to where Maggie disappeared to all the time. And she still had no desire to know.

"Are you worried Maggie will send you out working with Jane?" asked Jack. He took out the diamond-studded hatpin he had stolen that day and pressed it into her hand. "Take this. It'll keep her off your back."

Mary took it gratefully, offering her brother a small smile. Now sixteen, Mary knew she was lucky Maggie had not yet sent her out into the streets to sell herself to men. But Jack always gave her the most expensive things he stole each day. Pieces, he said, that would convince Maggie of Mary's value as a thief. Convince her that she should not be sent out to do even more demeaning work. Mary was eternally grateful to her brother. She slipped the pin into her pocket, flashing him a smile of thanks.

"It's not that," she admitted. "It's just... Christmas. I hate this time of year."

The horrors of last Christmas were still fresh in her mind. She never stopped thinking about the look of despair on Rose and Catherine's faces as

Maggie banished them from the tenement. She never stopped thinking about the pistol beneath Maggie's skirts, and the look of wild anger in her eyes.

Most of all, she never stopped thinking about Bobby. She knew there was little chance he had survived. In all likelihood, cholera would have taken him in days, if not hours. But that was a truth that was too hard to swallow. To make it easier, Mary would tell herself tales of where Bobby might be now. Perhaps he had recovered and had found honest work in the factories. Or perhaps a well-to-do family had found him on the street and taken him in to nurse him back to health. Tales she refused to look too hard at, in case the illusion crumbled.

Jack threw some kindling on the fire and struck a match. "I hate Christmas too." He sat back on his heels, watching the flames begin to lick the wood.

Mary sat beside him, hugging her knees. "We need to get out of here," she said suddenly. Though the thoughts of escape had been bubbling inside her for almost a year, it was the first time she had spoken of them aloud.

Jack looked at her with raised eyebrows. "And go where?"

Mary shrugged. The words had fallen out of her mouth without her having any thought of it. She had no idea where they would go. This place had been her home for the past six years. Maggie and the others were the closest to a family they had. Beyond those terrifying first few months before Maggie had found them at Covent Garden and taken them home to the tenement, they had never been alone.

But Mary was suddenly determined. "I don't know where we'll go," she admitted. "But we can't stay here. Just think about it, Jack. When we first got here there was twelve of us. And now Lizzie's left to marry that awful client of hers, there's less than half of that now. And apart from Lizzie, all the others are…"

Jack nodded slowly. Mary knew she didn't need to finish the sentence. *Couldn't* bring herself to finish it.

All the others are gone. Dead.

How long would it be before she and Jack were among them?

"I know you're right," said Jack. "We do need to get out. It's only a matter of time before something dreadful happens to us too. But we can't just run out into the street with no plan. Especially not at this time of year when it's so cold."

After a moment, Mary nodded. She knew her brother was right. She turned to face him, looking into his eyes. "But we'll make a plan," she said determinedly. "Won't we?"

"Yes," said Jack. "We will."

The door clicked open unexpectedly. Maggie stepped into the room and the siblings fell into silence.

"Merry Christmas, all of you," Maggie crowed brightly the next morning. Mary curled up on her sleeping pallet, gritting her teeth. Every Christmas morning she had spent with Maggie, she had made the same enthusiastic greeting, no matter what else was happening. No matter whether David and Brian were about to be hanged, or whether Tracy had failed to return home, or if Bobby and Rose and Catherine had been thrown out to the street to succumb to cholera.

"Merry Christmas, Maggie," said Harry, giving her a small smile.

Maggie stood in the centre of the room, hands planted on her hips. "What in hell's the matter with you all? You look as though somebody died! It's Christmas Day! Have you forgotten what that means? The greatest feast of the year!" She picked up the gin bottle from beside her rocking chair and took an enormous swig. "Wait til you see what I got for you all this year. A great big goose and every type of vegetable you can imagine. A goose! And maybe a little plum pudding if you bring me some treasures back from the church this morning."

Jack gave a strained smile. "Sounds delicious."

"Course it does." Maggie stepped close to Jack and put her hands on his shoulders. "I'm counting on you, young lad. You're the best thief I got. You're gonna bring me the goods today, ain't you?"

"I'll try," said Jack, avoiding Mary's eyes.

Maggie folded her arms. "Right then. You lot best get going. Get your Sunday best on and off to the church with you. It's a golden time for picking pockets, it is. Everyone's too busy wishing each other a merry Christmas to be bothered with looking out for thieves."

Glumly, Mary pulled on the fine wool dress Maggie had given her especially for this ruse at the church. Mary was a young woman now, Maggie had said, and to blend into the church crowd, she would need to look the part. Gone were the days when she could sneak around the city unnoticed as a filthy little street urchin. Now she was a pretty young woman of sixteen, she had to act like a young lady.

Mary said little as she walked with Jack and Harry towards the church at Spitalfields. Her thoughts were on the conversation with her brother the previous night. Escape was their only option. But how? Mary knew that if she dared to leave the relative safety of the tenement, it would only be a matter of time until she was standing on a street corner selling her body. And without Maggie's ability to bribe the police, there was every chance Jack would end up walking to the hangman.

As desperate as she was to leave, they could not just go charging out into the night with no place to go. She needed a plan. And somehow, she would come up with one.

The church was a wash of colour; women in bright gowns, and men in vibrant silk scarves and waistcoats. She did look the part, Mary thought, in her blue woollen dress and dark bonnet and Jack and Harry both in charcoal-coloured suits. No one would ever have guessed they were thieves. The three sidled towards the crowd.

Mary glimpsed a gold comb in the hair of the woman in from of her. Easy pickings. She felt the familiar stab of guilt that always came moments before she stole anything. But as she always did, she pushed it aside, snatching the comb as she pretended to bump into the woman. Mary gushed her apology, sliding the comb into her pocket and hurrying into the church.

She sat with Jack and Harry in a pew towards the middle of the church. Though Mary longed to hide away in the back, her brother had convinced her that sitting in the middle of the crowd would allow them to blend in more efficiently. Mary knew he was right. But she couldn't help but feel that she didn't belong in such a place.

She had vague memories of attending church with her parents before Jack was born. But after her mother had died, her father had shown no interest in attending. The only time he ever spoke of God was to curse His name for taking his wife away.

Since her mother's death, the only time Mary ever set foot inside a church was to steal. And though she had little experience of God, she felt sure He could see everything. Every coin she slipped into her pocket. Every watch, every comb, every necklace. Sitting here among these decent people, listening to the vicar speak of the joys of the day, made Mary's stomach turn over with dread and self-loathing. She didn't belong here. No doubt she and the others would be punished some-how, just as they were every Christmas.

Mary was glad when the service ended and the congregation stood to file out of the church. Though she doubted Maggie would be satisfied with her producing nothing more than a single hair comb, Mary didn't care. If Maggie wanted more, she could damn well go out and steal it herself.

"Thief!"

The woman's cry made Mary's heart leap into her throat. She whirled around wildly, looking in the direction of the commotion. At the far end of the church, men were clustered around a blond-haired boy in a dark suit. Women pressed them-selves against the walls, trying to escape the chaos.

Mary heard herself cry out involuntarily.

Jack.

She tried to push her way through the crowd towards him, her thigh knocking hard against the edge of one of the pews and pain shooting down her leg.

"Mary." She felt a hand around her arm and spun around to see her brother standing before her, a look of panic on his face.

"Jack?" she gushed. "I thought you—"

"It's Harry they caught," he told her. "He went for a gentleman's pocket watch and weren't quick enough to get away."

Mary looked over at the crowd of people gathered around the thief. Yes, she saw now, it was Harry, with the same blond hair as her brother, and wearing the same dark suit. Impulsively, she threw her arms around Jack and squeezed tightly.

"Come on," he told her. "We need to leave. Right now."

Mary glanced back over her shoulder at Harry. How could they just leave him to face the authorities? Likely, to face the hangman.

"Mary." Jack's voice was firm. "Now. You know there's nothing we can do."

Mary shook herself out of her stupor, sparked to life by Jack's firm words. As she hurried towards the door, she wondered what had happened to that meek little boy of six Jack had been when they had first come to live with Maggie.

No, she knew well what had happened to him. That meek little boy had been washed away by a difficult life of thieving and dodging the law. It was not the life she wanted for her brother. And it was not the life she wanted for herself. Something had to change.

DINNER THAT NIGHT was a subdued affair. Though Maggie tried her best to raise everyone's spirits, lavishing them with food and gifts, the atmosphere around the table was heavy. As promised, the table was laid with an extravagant spread – as much food as there had been that first Christmas. Back then, there had been twelve of them and Mary had considered herself lucky to have but a few bites. Today, there were just four of them spread out across the rough wooden benches: Jack and Mary, Maggie, and Jane. Their plates were piled high, but Maggie was the only one eating.

When Mary and Jack had returned home from the church and told the others about Harry's arrest, Jane had burst into tears. But Maggie had merely shrugged.

"Come on now," she'd said, "these things

happen." She broke into a wide grin, revealing a chipped front tooth. "All the more food for us now." She looked at Jack. "And you might as well have the clothes I bought for Harry this year." She chuckled. "He ain't going to be needed them, is he."

Mary stared at her in disbelief. "You don't even care, do you? You don't care about Harry or any of the others we've lost. Are we nothing more to you than a means of making money?"

Maggie glared at her with such fire in her eyes Mary thought she was going to strike her. "You ungrateful wretch," she hissed. "After all I've given you and your brother, this is how you repay me? By accusing me of not caring about you all? Every year I put on this marvellous Christmas dinner for you, and every year I see you all in fine clothes—"

"You gave us the fine clothes so we could go out and steal for you!" Mary cried. "Don't pretend it were because you cared for us! Everything you've ever done, you've done for your own good."

Maggie's slap came before Mary could make sense of it. All she was aware of was the hot sting against her cheek, making her eyes water. Jack and Jane had stood wide-eyed behind her, neither daring to say a word.

And now, an hour later, here they were gathered around a Christmas table that was as still and silent as a grave. *As it deserves,* Mary thought to herself, her cheek still smarting from the slap. As far as she was concerned, Christmas was not a time to be celebrated. It was merely a time to mourn all that they had lost.

CHAPTER 8

*J*ack, Mary and Maggie stood huddled together beside a mound of earth in the pauper's graveyard. There was not so much as a headstone; nothing more than a crooked wooden cross marking the resting place of Jane Tuesday. Flurries of snow swirled around them, stinging Mary's cheeks. She felt dampness soaking through the holes in her boots. Beside her, Maggie stood wrapped in a thick woollen cloak, her hands tucked into dark fur-trimmed gloves.

Mary stared dry-eyed at the grave. She felt an ache deep inside her for the loss of Jane. The older girl had become a close friend to her, particularly in the four years since Bobby's death. But Mary was unable to cry. She had gone through this too many times now; this painful loss at Christmas time. Now it was almost to be expected. And it was as though she had constructed a barrier around her heart that prevented her from falling to pieces. She wished she could cry for Jane but Mary knew she had to stay strong. At this time of year more than any other. Yes, tragedy had already struck but Mary knew enough to know there could still be more trouble coming.

Influenza had taken hold of Jane with terrifying alacrity. She had fallen ill and passed away before Maggie was even aware of her sickness. Mary knew that, had Maggie not had the habit of disappearing for days at a time, Jane would have been thrown out onto the street to die, just like Bobby, Rose and Catherine.

Mary stepped forward and dropped a single red rose on the grave. Its vivid colour was stark against the snow and the black earth speckled beneath it.

"Very touching," said Maggie with a snort of laughter.

Mary gritted her teeth, forcing down her anger. She would not make a scene at Jane's grave. She could not bring herself to cry for her friend, but she could do her the honour of holding her rage at

Maggie inside. Jack reached over and gave her hand a quick squeeze.

"Right then," said Maggie, clapping her hands together as she had done so many times around the supper table. "Let's get moving. We've got plans to make, my friends. And now it's just the three of us, so we all need to play our part." She shot venomous eyes at Mary.

Just the three of us.

The words stung.

Two years ago as she had watched Harry get hauled away by the police, Mary had sworn she would find a way out of Maggie's clutches. And yet here they were, with another Christmas upon them, mourning yet another loss.

And once again, Maggie had hatched a plan that would put wealth in her own pocket while putting Jack and Mary firmly in the path of the authorities.

This year, her plan revolved around a jeweller close to St Paul's Cathedral. Maggie would visit the jeweller in her finest clothes and pretend to be searching for a gift for her mother. She would slide a few pieces into her pockets while she browsed, only for Jack and Mary to then burst through the door with the pistol and demand all the money from the till.

When she had first heard of the plan, Mary had been terrified. This was no petty thieving. If they were caught, they would be locked up for life – if they were lucky enough to escape the hangman.

Maggie had laughed off her concerns. "There ain't nothing to be afraid of," she'd said. "We ain't fools. We all know what we're doing. 'Specially young Jack here." She winked at him. "Besides, we'll do this just before everything closes up for Christmas Eve. There'll be plenty of money in the till, plus everyone will have their minds on their celebrations. No one will be expecting a thing. No one gets caught at Christmas."

Mary looked at her pointedly. "What about Harry?" she asked. "He got arrested on Christmas morning. And what about David and Brian?"

Maggie sighed dramatically as though Mary were mad for mentioning their names. "They were all amateurs," she said. "You two, you know what you're doing. That's why you survived so long."

"I'm worried about tomorrow," Mary murmured to Jack as they trudged through the snow on their way home from the graveyard. "If we're caught waving a pistol around, we'll be hanged for certain."

"We won't get caught," said Jack. "It's like Maggie says, we know what we're doing."

But Mary could hear the thinness in his words. She knew he was just trying to reassure her. And his words were doing anything but.

MARY WOKE the next morning with a thumping heart. This was it. The day of the robbery.

She sat up on her sleeping pallet to see that Maggie was not in the room. No doubt she'd been out all night, cavorting with strange men and spending the money she made from Mary and Jack's thieving.

Mary got to her feet and drew in a breath to steady herself. She and Jack would both need to be on their guard today. They would need to stay focused and alert at all times. It was the only way they would survive.

Mary lit the fire and hung the kettle on the hook above the grate. She took the half-eaten loaf of bread from the small shelf and broke off a piece each for her and Jack.

They ate slowly, sitting opposite each other at the long wooden table, their hands wrapped around tin cups filled with tea.

"All right, Jack," said Mary. "Let's go over the way things are going to happen today. We need to make sure there are no mistakes. I ain't going to the hangman on account of Maggie Shaw."

Jack nodded, his eyes dark and serious. Slowly, he went through each step of the robbery. They had spent most of the previous night talking about it, ensuring each step was committed to memory.

"And then," Jack finished, "we get away without anyone knowing a thing."

"Good." Mary took a sip of tea, the nerves in her stomach settling a little. Jack knew what he was doing. So did she. Though of course, they could not account for Maggie's behaviour, she and her brother were as ready as they would ever be.

Jack reached across the table to cover Mary's wrist with his hand. "It's going to be all right, Mary. I promise."

"Yes," Mary said, drawing in another long, steadying breath. "You're right. It is." She managed a smile and felt a warmth inside her when Jack smiled back.

As they were washing and dressing at the basin

later that afternoon, Maggie clattered into the apartment. One side of her dark hair was unpinned and hung in unbrushed curls around her shoulders. Mud was caked to the hems of her woollen skirts, and the smell of gin was clinging to her.

"Well, would you just look at the two of you?" she crowed. "All cleaned up and sparkling like a penny." She cackled loudly and reached beneath her skirt for her pistol. She tossed it to Jack, who caught it clumsily in both hands. "Now," she said. "Just need to get myself looking like a lady."

After splashing around ineffectually at the washbin for a few minutes, Maggie announced she was ready. Though she'd re-pinned her hair and scrubbed most of the dirt from her cheeks, her skirts were still filthy and her breath reeked of liquor. No one in their right mind would ever mistake her for a lady.

Still, Mary had learned that Maggie was not one to be argued with. And she had learned that there was to be no changing her mind. So when Maggie swung the door open and charged off down the stairs, Mary sucked in her breath and followed.

Maggie strutted off through the streets towards

St Paul's, the two siblings trailing. Jack's hand was lodged in his pocket, and Mary imagined his fingers wrapped tightly around the pistol. She hated the thought of her little brother with a weapon in his hand.

The sun was beginning to sink behind the horizon, painting long shadows over the streets. The scent of roasting chestnuts hung in the air, reminding Mary of her and Jack's run-in with the fat man in Kensington so many Christmases ago.

Mary could see the jeweller on the corner. It was a small, unassuming shop, though its window was lavishly decorated with finely crafted jewellery. No doubt that at this time on Christmas Eve, their till would be overflowing.

Maggie stopped walking and turned to face the others. She spoke in a whisper. "All right? We all know what we're doing?"

Mary nodded. "Yes. Once we see you speaking to the jeweller, we'll come in and hold the place up."

"Good. Now off you two go and hide yourselves." Maggie grinned broadly, her blue eyes flashing. And for a second, she looked so wild that Mary couldn't help but fear her.

* * *

MAGGIE STRUTTED INTO THE JEWELLER, lifting her chin and giving an elaborate flick of her cloak as she entered.

Oh, this was an enjoyable game, pretending to be a lady and stealing from under these toffs' noses. And if something went wrong? Well, it wasn't her who would go to the gallows now, was it? She wasn't the one with the pistol in her hand. Not today. That was little Jack Talbot.

Maggie couldn't deny she'd be a little sad if Jack was to go to the hangman. He'd become her favourite of all those brats she'd taken under her wing over the years. And he'd become a fine thief too.

Yes, she thought, far better if it were to be that ungrateful sister of his. Who did she think she was, mouthing off the way she did like she was the queen herself? Mary Talbot wouldn't last two minutes out in this world alone. It was high time she started showing a little gratitude.

"Can I help you, ma'am?" the jeweller asked Maggie, stepping out from behind the counter.

"Yes. I like to inspect these rings," she said,

putting on her most polished accent. "A Christmas gift for my dear sister."

"Of course, ma'am."

What was that look the jeweller was giving her? A look that was disturbingly close to derision. As though he could somehow sense that tonight Maggie would be going home to a Whitechapel tenement instead of a grand townhouse in Mayfair.

Maggie snorted. What did this man know about who she was? Who was he to judge her? When he placed the array of gold rings in front of her, she swiftly slid one into her pocket.

"Oh, yes," she crowed, as the jeweller walked her through each of his creations. "I see." And then, just because of the look he had given her, she said, "Oh, no, I don't like that one at all. I've seen far nicer pieces in the jeweller's on Gray's Inn Road."

The man said nothing, just stepped back to allow Maggie to peruse the selection. When he wasn't looking, she snatched another ring.

She heard footsteps crunching through the snow.

Good, she thought. Mary and Jack were coming to hold the place up. She'd had about enough of this no-good toff who couldn't make a decent ring if his life depended on it. She spun around, ready to face Jack's pistol and launch into her finest acting display.

But the cry of shock that escaped her lips was genuine.

For it was not Mary and Jack in the doorway, but two policemen with wooden truncheons in hand. The taller of the two stepped towards her and reached into her pocket, pulling out the two rings she had swiped from the display.

"Maggie Shaw," he said, "you're under arrest." He stepped forward, pinning her arms behind her back.

Maggie's head swam. These policemen knew who she was? How was that possible? But when she peered through the window into the street, she saw Jack and Mary Talbot standing outside the jeweller's with smiles of victory on their faces.

CHAPTER 9

*M*ary held her breath as Maggie was led from the jeweller and towards the waiting police wagon. Her heart was racing.

"Ungrateful wretch!" Maggie hollered as she passed. "You'll be lost without me, Mary Talbot."

Mary allowed herself a faint smile. She knew that wasn't true. The prospect of a life without Maggie in it was a fine one.

Up until the last minute, she had feared she would not have the courage to go through with the plan; a plan she and Jack had concocted late one night when they were alone in the room. For eight years she had felt so powerless against Maggie. She was afraid she might not have the fortitude to go for the police. But when the time had come, she'd had no doubt.

As she and Jack had followed Maggie through the city on the way to the jeweller's, Mary had kept note of where police officers were patrolling. The moment Maggie had disappeared inside the shop, Mary had sprinted to the western edge of the cathedral to fetch the officers.

As the police wagon rolled away, Jack let out a whoop of delight. He threw his arms around Mary. "It worked! It really worked!"

Mary grinned. "It had to work," she said. "We planned everything out so carefully. She glanced up at the clock atop the cathedral. "Come on. There's still plenty more to do. We've got to get to the bank before it closes. I couldn't bear to spend another Christmas in that dreadful tenement."

She began to stride through the snow, Jack skipping to keep up with her.

"Now remember," Mary told him as they walked, "my name is Anne Davey. And you are my footman."

Jack took off his hat and dropped into a mock bow. "At your service, madam."

Mary grinned. She felt alive with optimism – a feeling she wasn't sure she had ever had before.

On Christmas Day two years ago, on the day of Harry's arrest, Mary had started making her plans for escape. And those plans had circled around Maggie Shaw.

Mary had always known there were things Maggie was keeping from them. Her band of thieves had always been profitable, even when their numbers began to dwindle. How was it possible, Mary had wondered, that they could afford no more than their leaky room in the tenement given the sheer amount of jewels and coin they stole for Maggie each day. Yes, they had coal and fire, and yes they managed a lavish dinner each Christmas, but for the rest of the year they ate nothing better than stew and stale bread. Meanwhile, Maggie's supply of gin seemed never-ending, and her clothes were always of the finest quality.

On the day after Harry's arrest, Mary had taken to following Maggie in secret. She followed her out of the tenement late at night and watched her mingle with men in taverns and opium dens. Watched her go to the pawnshops and sell off the goods the children had stolen.

And she watched her pocket far more money than was needed for the rent and upkeep of their room at the tenement.

Then Mary followed her to Glyn and Co bank on Lombard Street

Gaining the details of the safe deposit box was difficult. Mary had to follow Maggie into the bank itself; had to hide within the crowd in order to overhear her speaking to the gentleman behind the counter. And it was there that Mary learned of Anne Davey, Maggie's alter-ego, who had a more than sizeable sum hidden within the vaults of the bank.

At first, she had not planned on sending the police after Maggie. After all, despite everything she had done, Maggie had taken her and Jack in off the street and given them food and shelter. But when Maggie had presented the idea of the jeweller's robbery – a plan that would in all likelihood see both Mary and Jack hanged – Mary had done what she had to do.

Despite everything, Mary had expected a tiny pang of guilt when she watched Maggie get hauled away by the police. But there was none of that. Instead, all she thought of were the other children from the thieving ring; children whose deaths she held Maggie responsible for.

She thought of David and Brian, bold and over-confident, but always willing to protect the younger children. She thought of warm, kind-hearted Tracy and Jane Tuesday who had such high hopes of somehow finding a better life. She thought of Rose and Catherine and Harry.

Most of all, she thought of dear Bobby Taylor, who still had her heart four long years after his death.

It was her lost friends that had inspired Mary to act, just as much as it was her need to get out and make a better, safer life for her and her brother. And that life was almost within reach.

Mary's heart began to pound as they entered the bank. What if Maggie had sent the police after them in retaliation? Or what if there was something she hadn't considered; something that would see her revealed as an imposter?

She shook the thought away. There was no time for doubt now, no time for uncertainty. She had spent the past two years preparing for this moment. Trailing Maggie without being spotted, memorising the details of the safe deposit box, and practising her most refined accent. Dressed in her finest worsted gown, she knew she looked the part.

She lifted her chin and approached the counter, Jack trailing her with his eyes down. "I would like to withdraw the contents of my box," she told the man behind the counter, forcing a steadiness into her voice.

"Of course, ma'am. Name?"

"Anne Davey. Date of birth…" Mary recited the rest of the details, feeling her shoulders sink in relief when the man said,

"This way, ma'am. Follow me."

She followed him deep into the bank, through the dimly-lit passages behind the foyer. Jack hurried along behind them, keeping his eyes to the floor. Their footsteps echoed on the cold stone floor. Mary's heart was beating so loudly in her ears that she was sure her brother could hear it.

"Here we are. Number three-six-seven."

The man stepped forward and unlocked the safe.It was one of the largest of the boxes available. As the heavy door swung open, Mary stifled a cry of surprise. The safe was crammed with more riches than she had dared imagine. Boxes were stacked up neatly, and from her previous spying escapades, Mary knew them to be filled with coins. Various pieces of jewellery were laid out beside the boxes. Sitting in one corner, she glimpsed a fine ruby necklace she remembered stealing from outside a teahouse in Covent Garden many years ago. She had imagined Maggie had sold it right away, using the money for rent. But she could see now how naïve she had been back then. The sale of the necklace alone would have kept them in the tenement for months.

"You wish to withdraw the entire contents, ma'am?"

"Yes. Thank you. Please put the jewellery in my reticule. My footman will carry the boxes."

"Of course, ma'am." The man moved swiftly, filling the embroidered reticule Mary had stolen from Maggie that morning. There was something delightfully ironic, she thought to herself, about using Maggie's bag to transport years' worth of her stolen goods.

The man passed her the reticule and Mary nodded her thanks. Tried to hide her smile of excitement at the thought of what might come next.

CHAPTER 10

*M*ary and Jack woke up on Christmas morning in Mirvart's Hotel. Using the money she had withdrawn from Maggie's safe, Mary had booked the top floor suite – a lavish collection of rooms with enormous, cloudlike canopy beds, fine wooden furniture, and three separate fireplaces. This Christmas, she told herself, they would really have something to celebrate. Mary had booked the suite of rooms for a week, guessing it was enough time for them to make their plans for the future. The cost of the rooms had barely made a dent in the vast expanse of Maggie's fortune.

Our fortune, Mary thought with a smile as she

lay on her back in the palatial bed, pulling the thick blankets to her chin. She could hear Jack's footsteps pattering around in the next room.

She slid out of bed and dressed quickly, splashing her face at the washstand. Despite the luxurious comfort of the bed, she had found it difficult to get to sleep. Her thoughts had been whirring with nerves and excitement for much of the night. With the money in her hands, the future lay ahead of her, full of possibilities. What would it be like to live like a wealthy person, instead of a penniless orphan with no choice but to pick pockets? Mary could hardly make sense of it. It was as though the girl she had been her entire life had suddenly been swept away. And while it was a dizzying, unmoored feeling, it brought her no end of happiness.

She dressed quickly, then knocked on Jack's door. When he called out to her in greeting, she poked her head inside.

"Good morning!" he beamed. "Merry Christmas!"

The sight of him standing atop the enormous bed with his arms outstretched made Mary burst into joyful laughter. Never in her wildest dreams had she imagined herself and her brother in a place such as this. But yes, she thought with a grin, the high life suited Jack.

She rushed forward and pulled her brother off the bed, drawing him into a tight embrace. "Merry Christmas, Jack!"

Jack squeezed her tightly and then took a step back. "Can you believe this place?" he gushed. "We're living like kings and queens. I'm certain my bed is the size of the entire room back in Whitechapel."

"Best you get used to it," Mary told him with a grin. "This is our life now!"

Jack ran over to the window and pulled back the heavy velvet curtain. Bright sunlight flooded the room.

Mary stood beside her brother and looked down over the street. Fresh snow had fallen during the night, blanketing the world in a brilliant white. Carriages carved their way through the glittering streets, their wheels leaving neat black trails behind them. Despite the snow, people clustered the footpaths, colourful in their Sunday best as they greeted each other with handshakes, waves and warm greetings. From high up in the hotel suite, they looked like little more than toys.

From somewhere below, Mary could hear the

gentle melodies of carollers rising to meet them. "I wish the others could have experienced this," she said, resting her forehead against the cool glass.

Jack nodded. "I know. So do I. They deserved it." He reached for Mary's hand and gave it a small squeeze. "But today is Christmas Day. And it's about time we had a Christmas that was worthy of celebrating."

And celebrate, they did. The Christmas lunch served at the hotel put even the most lavish of Maggie's spreads to shame. Their table was laden with roast beef, and chestnut-stuffed turkey, oyster soup, and potatoes mashed with onions. There was Yorkshire pudding and fillets of fish, and bowls and bowls of vegetables. Many of the dishes, Mary had never seen before, and she had little idea of what she was eating. She didn't care. Today was a day of celebration. Today was the start of the rest of their lives.

Jack took an enormous bite of plum pudding and let out a groan of satisfaction. "This is so good, Mary. You have to try it."

Mary grinned, looking down at the bowl of pudding before her, lashed with a generous helping of cream. Though she wanted nothing more than to swallow every scrap, she had eaten so much meat and vegetables she could barely fathom taking another bite. Nonetheless, she took a tiny portion onto her spoon and swallowed it down. Jack was right. It was utterly delicious.

"What do you think you will do?" Jack asked her, his spoon held in mid-air. "Now we're free?"

Mary took a long breath. *Free.* The word felt foreign. And so did the feeling. They had the money to do almost anything they wanted. They could travel the world, or buy a fine house in London, or a mansion overlooking the ocean... It was all so overwhelming.

"I don't know," she admitted. "I've never thought about what I would do if... well... if I could do anything I wanted." For as long as she could remember, her life had just been about survival. About ensuring she and Jack had a roof over their head and food in their bellies. About ensuring they both avoided the hangman.

Jack nodded. "I know. It's almost a little scary."

Mary nodded. But it was scary, she realised, in the best of ways.

"I'd like a business of my own," Jack said suddenly. "Where I make the decisions and can live my life the way I want to." He shifted forward on his chair, his eyes alight with enthusiasm. "And I'd make sure that everyone that works for me was treated real good. Got to go home in time to eat supper with their families. Got to stay home when they're sick."

Mary smiled, feeling a sudden rush of pride for her little brother. How, she wondered, had he grown up to be such a thoughtful young man when he had lived the life he had. Perhaps it was thanks to that life, she thought. She and Jack had seen the worst life had to offer. They had seen the worst in humanity – and that drove them both to want to be far better people. She would use this money for good, Mary decided then. Stolen money, yes, but perhaps in her hands, it could become a force for good. She would give to those who needed it. Help children like her off the streets. Perhaps that would go some way to making up for all the lives that had been lost during the creation of Maggie's fortune.

She looked back at her brother. "I think you'd make a wonderful business owner," she said. "Anyone would be lucky to work for you."

Jack beamed and sat straighter in his chair. And

at that moment, Mary saw him not as the scruffy younger brother he had always been but as a fine young man with a bright future ahead of him. In a few months, Jack would be fifteen, and Mary knew with certainty that he would make his mark on the world.

"What about you?" he asked, flashing her a teasing grin. "Will you find yourself some rich toff to marry?"

"What do I need a rich toff for?" laughed Mary. "I'm the one with all the money."

She told Jack then about her need to do good with money. Her need to make amends for all the crimes she had committed throughout her life – including the burglary of Maggie's safe.

Jack looked across the table to meet her eyes. "You're a good person, Mary. You know that, don't you?"

Mary looked down. She didn't feel like a good person. She wasn't sure she ever had.

Jack reached over and touched her wrist, forcing her to look at him. "You've always been so kind and caring. Not just to me, but to all the other orphans too. We were all so lucky to have you." He lowered his voice a little. "I know we haven't lived the most honest, decent life, but that can change now."

Mary smiled. Her brother was right. "Yes," she said, scooping up another spoonful of pudding. "It can. And it will."

"So," said Jack, leaning back in his chair. "Maggie was richer than I could believe. Why do you think she still lived in the tenement?"

Mary sighed. She had asked herself that question many times since she had first discovered the existence of the vault.

"We were Maggie's way of making money," she said. "She hardly did any of the thieving herself. It was all of us that made her rich. She needed us around."

Jack nodded. "Still, that tenement was a dreadful place to live. Why do you think she stayed there so long?"

Mary chewed her lip. "Honestly, I think Maggie was quite mad."

"I think she was too," Jack said quietly.

"I truly don't know what else would explain it," Mary continued. "No one in their right mind would choose to live in that place." She thought of all the horrid clubs and taverns she had seen

Maggie visit throughout the two years she had followed her. Thought of all the vile men and women she associated with. "No one would have done the things she did if they were in their right mind."

For the first time, Mary wondered about Maggie's past. Was she an orphan, like the children they had lived in the tenement with? Had she been beaten by her father, as Mary had been? Or been taken from the workhouse like Jane Tuesday? Had she ever had to sell her body, like Tracy and Lizzie? Perhaps. Mary knew that, in all likelihood, Maggie had suffered just as much as the rest of them. But none of that, she thought bitterly, made up for what she had done.

None of it made up for her sending Tracy out to be murdered or throwing Bobby and the girls out into the street to die of cholera. And none of it made up for the fact that every day of the past eight years, she had sent them all out to steal for her, so she might fill her vault with riches.

"I want to give them all proper graves," Mary said suddenly. "Somewhere we can go to remember them. Not just Jane, who was buried in that awful pauper's grave, but all of them. David and Brian and Tracy... Everyone we've lost. This money belongs to them as much as it does us." Her voice wavered slightly, as she was struck with a sudden wave of emotion. "I know there's little we can do for them now. But we can do this."

Jack gave her a small smile. "I know they would appreciate that."

Mary sniffed, wiping away a stray tear. "The rest of the world just forgets about people like us. We just die on the streets, or we're hanged, or murdered by clients, and no one thinks twice about it. We ain't worth nothing to no one." Her voice wavered. "But I'm gonna make sure none of our friends are ever forgotten."

Jack raised his wine glass. "To our friends."

Mary smiled through her tears, clinking her glass against his. "To our friends."

* * *

Several hours later, Mary and Jack made their way back up to their rooms. Mary's cheeks felt pleasantly warm from the wine, her full stomach pressing against her corset.

"That meal was amazing," Jack sighed happily. "Much better than anything Maggie ever laid out."

Mary pulled the key from her reticule and unlocked the door to their suite. The living area was comfortably warm and a young hotel worker was crouching over the hearth to restoke the fire.

"Oh," Mary gushed, "it's so lovely and warm in here. Thank you."

"Of course, ma'am." The worker got to his feet and turned to face Mary.

She froze, her body going suddenly hot and then cold. No, it couldn't be. How was this possible? "Bobby?" she managed.

His lips parted in shock before a wide smile spread across his face. "Mary? Is it really you?"

Mary rushed forward and threw her arms around him, squeezing tightly. She felt tears of happiness welling behind her eyes. She stepped back, gripping his forearms, keeping him close to her. Bobby looked just as she remembered, with a stray lock of brown hair falling across his forehead and the same hint of a dimple in one cheek. But his dark eyes were alight, and his skin had a healthy glow. "How...? I thought you..."

Bobby gave a gentle laugh. "I could ask the same of you! Whoever would have thought I'd find young Mary Talbot up here in our finest suite?" He looked over at Jack, giving him a warm smile. "It seems the two of you have come quite a way in the world."

Mary let out her breath, pulling him close again. "Oh, Bobby, I've got so much to tell you." Her tears spilt, and she let them fall unhindered onto her lace collar.

"I've got so much to tell you, too," he said, squeezing her hands. "I'm due to finish work in an hour. Perhaps I might come back then?"

Mary could do little more than nod through her joyful tears. "Of course," she managed. "Of course. Come whenever you can."

Bobby gave her hands a final squeeze and then headed towards the door. He looked back over his shoulder at Mary. He gave her a smile that seemed to reach deep inside, warming her to the core and thawing so many years of bitterness.

As the door thumped closed behind him, Mary dropped to her knees in disbelief. Bobby Taylor, her dearest friend. The young man she had spent the past four years mourning. Alive.

There was no other day in the year, Mary thought with a joyful sob, that she loved more than Christmas.

MARY SPENT the next hour pacing back and forth across the living area. Her mind was racing, trying to find an answer to how Bobby had ended up here. She had never dared to dream this. Not once had she ever truly allowed herself to imagine that Bobby might be alive. It was far too painful.

But now footsteps were clicking rhythmically in the hallway outside the suite. Bobby's footsteps. He knocked lightly on the door, making Mary's heart skip a beat.

Jack flashed his sister a smile. "I'll be in my room if you need me." He disappeared around the corner before she could speak.

She opened the door to find Bobby with a warm smile on his face. He was still wearing his neat black uniform and was clutching a small china jug.

"I brought cocoa," he said. "I hope it's still your favourite."

Mary burst into tearful, joyous laughter. "Yes," she managed. "Yes, Bobby, it's still my favourite."

She took a step back, allowing him to enter the suite. Bobby set the jug on the table and took two cups from the sideboard. He filled them each to the brim, the delicious aroma making Mary's mouth water, despite having had the enormous lunch.

She and Bobby sat down together at the table, their knees inches apart. For several long moments, they just stared at each other, caught in disbelief.

Mary reached out and took Bobby's hand in both of hers. "How are you here?" she asked throatily. "When Maggie threw you out into the street, I was so sure you..." she faded out, unable to finish. "You survived," she managed.

Bobby gave her fingers a gentle squeeze. "Yes. I did." His thumb moved gently over the top of her hand. "Rose and Catherine, they were much sicker than I was. After Maggie threw us out, we ended up in an alley on the edge of the slums. The girls were too sick to stand, and in the morning, they were both dead." His voice was thin, and Mary could tell it was still difficult for him to speak about.

She felt her own throat tighten at the thought of the two young girls' lives ending in the middle of a Whitechapel alley. Rose and Catherine had deserved far better.

"I didn't know what to do," Bobby continued. "I didn't want to just leave them there, but I had no thought of what to do. So I went to the church at Spitalfields."

The church where Harry was caught, Mary thought distantly.

"I told the vicar that my two friends had died in the alley," Bobby said. "He told me he would take care of them. I'm not sure if I believed him." He sniffed. "I wanted to, but…"

"But it always felt like we were worth nothing," Mary finished.

Bobby nodded. "As I was leaving the church, I heard someone calling to me. There was an old woman in the church, praying. She must have heard my conversation with the vicar. She asked me where I was going." His voice wavered slightly at the memory. "I told her to stay away from me. I didn't want to make her sick. But she wouldn't listen. She asked me if I had somewhere to go, and I admitted that I didn't."

Mary looked into Bobby's eyes and saw they were gleaming with tears.

"She took me home with her," he said, his voice wavering. "Even though I was sick. She told me it was the right thing to do, and that it was what God would want. I couldn't believe it. I'd never known that sort of kindness. She took me home and gave me a bed and some clean clothes. Fed me, and looked after me until I was strong again. Her son and her husband had both died many years ago, and she was all alone, just like I was. I think perhaps we both needed each other." He smiled. "A year and a half ago, she helped me get this job. I still live with her, in a little townhouse in Clerkenwell."

Mary wiped away her tears. Her heart swelled with gratitude for the nameless old woman who had brought Bobby back to her. His fingers were warm in hers, and she gave them a gentle squeeze. Never wanted to let go.

"I never forgave Maggie," she admitted, her eyes on their interlaced fingers.

"She did what she had to," Bobby said. "She was right – if we had have stayed in the tenement, we would have made you all sick."

Mary shook her head. "It wasn't just what she did to you. It was what she did to all of them." In a husky voice, she told Bobby about those they had lost since he had left the tenement. Told him about Harry's arrest, and Jane's illness and the miserable pauper's grave where her body lay. But her bitter anger at Maggie had begun to fade a little, Mary realised. The anger was still there, but it didn't feel quite so consuming. How could she feel rage when Bobby had been returned to her?

"Well," she said, straightening her shoulders, "I suppose we have Maggie to thank for finding each other again."

Bobby raised his eyebrows. "How so?"

And, sipping from her cup of cocoa, Mary told him everything; about following Maggie across the city for two years and discovering the existence of the safe deposit box. And about Maggie's attempted burglary of the jeweller's, and the way Mary had sent the police after her.

"And then," she finished, "I went to the bank myself. Pretended I was Maggie and took every scrap out of that safe."

Bobby's eyes were shining. He began to laugh. "Mary Talbot, you cunning little thing. I'm so proud."

He dived forward suddenly, pressing his lips into hers. He pulled away at once. "I'm sorry," he garbled. "I didn't…"

Mary shook her head. "Don't be sorry. At all." She felt warmth rising in her cheeks and filling her chest. She leaned forward, kissing Bobby gently, tasting the cocoa on his lips.

His knees pressing against hers, he ran a gentle finger down her cheek. "Where will you go from here?" he asked.

"I don't know," Mary admitted. The world felt impossibly vast. And alive with possibilities. "But I can't wait to find out."

EPILOGUE

Mary hung the last of the ribbons on the Christmas tree and stepped back to admire her work. Though the tree was small, it was neat and symmetrical, brightly decorated with red and gold ribbons, and strings of coloured beads. It looked perfect sitting in front of the wide windows of their parlour, looking out onto the snow-lined street.

After marrying several months before, Mary and Bobby had purchased a townhouse in a fine street in Kensington. A street that had felt oddly familiar to Mary at the time; a familiarity she was unable to place. It was only on her way home from the market one day that she had been able to place it.

Stepping out from the house next door to hers was an overweight man and his elegant blonde wife. Though it had been almost nine years since she had last seen them, Mary recognised them at once. On Christmas Eve, back when she was a ten-year-old child, she had peered through their window at a dining table laden with food.

At the sight of them, she was taken back to that night; a night of tearing across London, being chased by the fat man's butler. How narrowly she and Jack had escaped...

When she had told Bobby over dinner that night, a frown had creased the bridge of his nose.

"How do you feel about living next door to them?" he had asked. "They were the ones who caught Brian and David."

Mary nodded. "I know." At first, that was all she could think about. Would she be able to walk past the man's house without thinking of her two friends facing the hangman? But then she realised she had been looking at things the wrong way. Living next to the fat man and his wife should not remind her of all the terrible things that had happened in the past. It should remind her of how far she had come. Remind her that that past was behind her and that she had a wonderful new life ahead of her.

When she told Bobby this, he reached across the table and squeezed her hand. "I'm glad you feel that way."

"Just promise me one thing," said Mary. "That we'll never become like that family. Stuffing ourselves with more food than we need, and sending the police after street urchins that come to our door."

Bobby shifted in his chair so that he was closer to her. "Mary," he said, meeting her eyes, "I know with all my heart that that will never happen. You are far too kind and decent. You care so much about other people." He leaned forward and kissed her gently. "I know nothing in the world will change that."

Since that night, the sight of the fat man and his wife always reminded her of Bobby's words. Always made her smile. And despite herself, she couldn't resist the occasional peek through the window, just for old time's sake.

The lock on the front door clicked open and Bobby's footsteps sounded down the hallway. He appeared at the door of the parlour.

"That tree!" he exclaimed. "It looks amazing!"

He made his way towards Mary, wrapping his arms around her and kissing her warmly.

She grinned. "I'm glad you like it."

He tucked a stray strand of hair behind her ear. "Whoever thought you'd come to love Christmas as much as you do?"

Mary pressed her hands against his cold cheeks. "How can I do anything but love Christmas when it was the day you came back to me?" She took his hands in hers. "Are you ready to go? Or would you like to rest a little before we go out again?"

"I'm ready to go out again," said Bobby. "Although Jack won't be joining us. He's held up at work. But he says he's to come to see us later tonight. He has something important to share with you."

On the day after Christmas the previous year, Jack had set in motion his dream of owning his own business. He had spent the year frequenting the coffee houses of London in order to make contacts and had pored over an endless array of books in order to improve his almost non-existent reading, writing and arithmetic skills. He had even hired a private tutor to visit him each morning.

These days, Jack's reading and writing were as fine as any young man's.

Last month, Bobby had left his position at Mirvart's Hotel, and he and Jack were in the process of establishing their new import-export business, in partnership with two of Jack's new contacts. Just as he had proclaimed he would be, Jack was now the proud owner of his own business – and Mary couldn't have been prouder.

She raised her eyebrows. "He has something important to share with me? What is it?"

Bobby gave her a playful grin, the dimple in his cheek deepening. "I promised him I wouldn't say. You'll find out later. Shall we go? I've brought the flowers you asked for. Nine red roses."

Mary nodded. "I'll get my coat."

They took a cab across town to Spitalfields. The city was alive on Christmas Eve; people hurrying back and forth between shops and markets, clutching baskets of food, or neatly wrapped toys. Christmas carols sung by a small choir reached them through the windows of the cab, as did the heady aroma of roasting chestnuts. There really was magic in the air at this time of year, Mary realised. It had just taken her a while to see it.

When they reached the church, Bobby leapt out of the cab, paid the coachman and then held out his hand to help Mary from the carriage.

"Careful now," he said. "It's a little icy."

Mary flashed him a warm smile. "It's all right, Bobby. I promise I won't break."

Bobby slid his arm around her as they began to walk. "I know you won't. You're far too strong for that. But that doesn't mean I don't want to take care of you."

They stepped through the gate of the church-yard and walked carefully through the snow to the graveyard. The memorial stones stood in a row at the back of the cemetery; one for each of their lost friends. Having them erected had been one of the first things Mary had done after taking the money from Maggie's vault. She had chosen to have them placed here at the church in Spitalfields, where the old woman had saved Bobby's life.

The memorial stones looked stark and oddly beautiful against the fresh snow. A fitting tribute to each of the lost orphans. Carefully, Mary walked along the row, placing a rose at the foot of each stone; David and Brian, Tracy, Rose, Catherine, Harry and Jane. At the end of the row, she placed two more flowers; one for Lizzie, who Mary hoped was safe and well with her husband. And the last rose for Maggie.

After her arrest, Maggie had turned violent and had been sent to Bethlem Hospital. Despite everything, Mary was glad she had not been hanged. And though she knew life at the asylum would not be easy, she felt certain it was where Maggie needed to be.

She stood close to Bobby, resting her head against his shoulder as they stood in silence by the memorial stones. Mary felt a deep peace settle over her. Though she would always mourn her lost friends, she was infinitely grateful for the turn her life had taken.

A light snow began to fall, settling on the tops of the gravestones. Mary shivered.

"Come on," said Bobby, giving her a squeeze. "We ought to get back. It's getting cold. And Jack will be over soon."

Mary nudged her husband playfully. "You're not going to tell me a thing about this surprise of his?"

Bobby grinned. "Not a word." He brought her gloved hand to his lips and kissed it. "Just as I didn't say a word to him about the surprise you have for him."

* * *

WHEN JACK APPEARED at the door of the townhouse later that evening, he was not alone. When the maid ushered him into the parlour, he was accompanied by a petite young woman, dressed in a dark green wool dress and matching coat. Blonde curls poked out from beneath her fur-trimmed bonnet.

Jack was shifting edgily from one foot to the other. "Mary," he said, "I'd like you to meet Elizabeth." His nervous eyes shifted to the young woman, and his face lit up suddenly. "She and I are to be married."

"Married?" Mary repeated in surprise. "Oh, Jack, that's wonderful!" She hurried to embrace her brother and offer warm greetings to Elizabeth.

The maid took Elizabeth's hat and coat, and the young couple sat side by side on the chaise beside the roaring fire.

"Tell me everything," said Mary. "How did you meet? And when?"

Jack told his sister the details, with his hand firmly clasped around Elizabeth's. Mary felt a warmth in her chest. How happy she was for her brother.

"This calls for a celebration," she said when Jack

had finished his story. She got to her feet. "I'm sure we've some champagne in the kitchen."

As she made her way down the passage, she heard footsteps behind her. Jack jogged up to join her. "Thought you could use some help carrying the glasses."

Mary smiled. "I'm so happy for you, Jack," she said as they walked. "She's wonderful."

Jack beamed. "She is wonderful. Truly. And I'm so glad you like her." He chuckled. "I was so nervous introducing you to her. Ask Bobby; I was a wreck at work today."

Mary shook her head, pushing open the door of the kitchen. "Were you truly so worried I wouldn't approve?"

"Not that you wouldn't approve of Elizabeth. But I know she and I are both young. And I've only just started to make my way in the world." His eyes shone. "But I love her, Mary. And I don't want to wait. If I learned anything during our time with Maggie, it's that life is precious. And we should make every moment count."

The warm feeling in Mary's chest swelled. "You're right," she said. "And you have my approval, Jack. You've always had it. I'm so proud of you."

He gave her a small smile. "Thank you. That means a lot."

Mary reached into the cupboard for the champagne glasses and set them on the sideboard. "I have some news of my own," she said, her eyes shining. "I'm with child. With God's grace, you'll be an uncle next Christmas."

Jack's face broke into an excited smile. He wrapped his sister in a tight embrace. "You deserve every happiness, Mary. I'm so pleased for you." He stepped back, giving her hand a quick squeeze. "Merry Christmas, Mary."

"Merry Christmas, Jack."

Printed in Great Britain
by Amazon

49541797R00079